HER FATHER'S DAUGHTER

HER FATHER'S DAUGHTER

June Tate

severn
House

This first world edition published 2012
in Great Britain and in the USA by
SEVERN HOUSE PUBLISHERS LTD of
9–15 High Street, Sutton, Surrey, England, SM1 1DF.
Trade paperback edition first published
in Great Britain and the USA 2013 by
SEVERN HOUSE PUBLISHERS LTD.

British Library Cataloguing in Publication Data

Tate, June.
  Her father's daughter.
  1. Southampton (England)–Social conditions–20th
  century–Fiction.
  I. Title
  823.9'2–dc23

ISBN-13: 978-0-7278-8203-5 (cased)
ISBN-13: 978-1-84751-451-6 (trade paper)

Except where ac
described for the
publication are f
is purely coincid

All Severn House ti

M
Pape
responsible
FSC FSC® C018575
www.fsc.org

Typeset by Palimpsest Book Production Ltd.,
Falkirk, Stirlingshire, Scotland.
Printed and bound in Great Britain by
MPG Books Ltd., Bodmin, Cornwall.

With love to my family.
Maxine, Beverley, Ronnie, Katie and Samantha.

One

Victoria Teglia sat in her office in the Club Valletta which was due to be opened the following day. She picked up the framed photograph of her late father who had died when she was a small baby and murmured, 'Well, Dad, what do you think? Does this meet with your approval?'

Carrying the picture she walked through the corridor into the main room of the club. The tables in the dining area were laid ready for the next day with damask tablecloths, cutlery, glasses and a low table decoration of small flowers. Running down one side of the room was a well-stocked bar, the bottles of spirits lined up on optics, the glass shelves gleaming beneath the many bottles displayed. There was a small area cleared for dancing and the stage dressed ready for the three-piece band that would play for the patrons on a Saturday night and on special occasions. At other times there would be a pianist or piped music in the background.

She opened the door leading into the gaming room. There were three roulette tables and other tables to be used for card games. She walked round checking that everything was in a pristine condition.

Returning to the bar, she poured a gin and tonic and sat on a bar stool, standing the photo where she could gaze at it. The steady expression of her father, Vittorio, once known as The Maltese, for that was where he was born, seemed to stare back at her.

'The club may carry the same name, Father dear, but it will be run very differently,' she muttered. 'There will be no brasses working here now and the gambling will be legitimate . . . What do you think about that, I wonder?' She raised a glass towards the photo and sipped the contents.

Vittorio Teglia had met his death in this building many years before – whilst Victoria was a baby – when he tried to save another man who was trapped in the blaze that had burnt out the upper storey. As a child, having been told this, Victoria had considered her father to be a hero, until she'd started school and been taunted about her late father by other pupils who had said he was a criminal. When she'd questioned her mother, Lily, about it she'd been fobbed off with various excuses until, as a teenager, her mother had taken her aside and told her the truth, when once again his past had been brought up by a girl she had thought of as a friend. She remembered the conversation clearly.

Victoria had returned home upset by the remarks and had been in tears at what she thought was an outrageous attack on the character of a man she had always considered so brave and courageous.

Taking her hand Lily said, 'It's time you knew the truth about your father, Victoria.'

The girl's heart sank.

'Your father died a hero and don't you ever forget that! But . . . he wasn't a saint. The Club Valletta was an exclusive establishment, used by the upper echelon of Southampton's society, the rich and wealthy used to go there all the time. They ate the finest food in the classiest surroundings, with staff to tend to their every need and, if they so wished, there were also hostesses to keep them company.'

Victoria looked horrified. 'Hostesses? Do you mean prostitutes? Did my father run a brothel?'

'Well, if you must be quite so blunt then – yes, he did. But the women were hand-picked by him. They were clean and many were well educated.'

'But that's illegal!' She was outraged. 'How could you love a man like that?'

'Oh, Victoria, how easy it is for you to sit in judgement! You have no idea how things were in those days. Your father took me in when I was in dire straits. I knew what he was as he never pretended to be anything else. He was intelligent, charming and he took care of me. I grew to love him deeply and when I became pregnant with you, he was delighted and when you were born, he idolized you. Had he lived, you would have loved him too.'

Victoria was speechless. The picture she'd carried with her of the man who'd fathered her – destroyed. She didn't know what to say for a minute. Then she asked, 'How did he get away with it?'

'Vittorio had friends in high places; many of them used the club in fact, so if the police were planning a raid, he was forewarned and so he kept ahead of the law. But nevertheless he was a man of principle, which may surprise you. He paid his bills on time, he looked after his staff – and he looked after me.' Seeing the stricken face of her daughter, she added, 'He wasn't a bad man, Victoria.'

In the years that followed, she had learned even more about her father's life mixing with the world of criminals. It worried her and fascinated her at the same time and now she was in partnership with George Coleman, who'd been Vittorio's right-hand man.

Coleman had been left a large sum of money in Vittorio's will as a reward for the years of loyalty he'd shown. He had given up a life of crime, had invested the money and, just before the end of the war a few months ago, had bought the building with the intention of opening up a new Club Valletta. When Victoria had returned from France as a member of the WRNS and wondering what the devil she was going to do once she'd been demobbed, he'd offered her a partnership.

She smiled slowly as she looked at the photo. How ironic it was. She was going down a similar path, but this time the law was on their side. She'd had to get the licence in her name as George did have a criminal record and, even though he'd been straight for a number of years, no way was the law going to allow him to hold the licence.

When Victoria had first told her mother of her plans, Lily had been concerned.

'I think the idea of a club is fine, but to call it by the same name I think is a big mistake! People have long memories. They won't remember your father's heroism, only that the club was run by The Maltese, one of Southampton's biggest villains and is now being reopened by his daughter. You'll end up as notorious as your father!' Angry words had been exchanged.

It was Luke Langford, Victoria's stepfather, who had calmed

Lily down when she told him of her concerns. He and Lily had been married when Victoria was a small child and they ran the Langford Hotel in Cumberland Place.

'It's different now, Lily,' he'd said. 'Times have changed. Besides, George wouldn't let any harm come to Victoria, she's as precious to him as Vittorio was. I don't see a problem here.'

Lily didn't argue further. Luke hadn't experienced the seedy side of life as she'd been forced to do. As the mistress of The Maltese, Lily had been witness to the workings of local gangsters trying to muscle in on Vittorio's territory, been aware of how such things had been dealt with. Oh no, she didn't want this for her daughter. Even though everything was supposed to run within the bounds of the law, who knows what would crawl out of the woodwork once it was known the daughter of The Maltese was in business now and in the same establishment? It was inevitable and she was filled with trepidation.

Early the following morning a reporter for *The Southern Evening Echo* called for an interview with the new owner of the club. He arrived with a photographer who had taken pictures of the interior. George had declined to be interviewed and had left Victoria to handle the young man. It wasn't long before the inevitable questions about Vittorio arose.

'Miss Teglia, will the new club be run on the same lines as when your late father owned it?' he asked with a sly grin.

Victoria looked him straight in the eye. 'Unfortunately my father died when I was a baby, so I have no idea how he ran his establishment, but Mr Coleman and I intend to offer an excellent menu, good service, a great ambience and a place that members can truly enjoy.'

'I see it's you who holds the license as it's your name over the door. Is this because Mr Coleman has a prison record?'

Victoria felt her hackles rise, but she remained calm and smiled. 'Young man, you are looking for a story to sell your paper and that's your job, I have a new business to sell and that's mine. I just hope we can keep this on a civilized level. I will be using your paper in the future to advertise, it would be a pity if you were the means of the paper losing this lucrative business because you decided to make a sensation out of nothing!'

He gazed at her with admiration. Here was a spirited young woman and he liked that. Closing his notebook he rose from his seat. Looking around he said, 'Well you've done a great job here, Miss Teglia, I wish you luck with the opening this evening.'

Victoria walked him to the door and shook his hand. 'I'll look forward to reading your report,' she told him.

George was waiting for her as he'd been listening. 'Cheeky young pup! I wanted to smack him one.'

'No more than I did!' she exclaimed, 'but we have a business to run and we don't want to be scuppered before we open.'

Invitations had been sent to all the major businessmen of the town inviting them to the grand opening night with a view to becoming a member. A uniformed doorman would stand guard for casual customers, sorting the wheat from the chaff and letting in only those he thought suitable as future patrons.

'I don't want any rough stuff,' Victoria warned him. 'I want you to be polite at all times, but firm with any undesirables. Do you understand?'

'Yes, miss.'

Eventually the doors were due to open for business. There was a great air of excitement among the hand-picked staff inside the club that night as they waited for the doors to open for the first time. Victoria felt sick in the pit of her stomach and went into the kitchen for a dry biscuit to nibble on.

With a look of sympathy, the chef handed her one. 'It'll be fine Miss Teglia, you'll see. The town needs a bit of excitement, the war has sapped everyone and now they want to enjoy themselves. You wait; we'll be packed out before the night's end!' And he was right.

No sooner had the doors opened, people started arriving. Some came because it was a new venture; others, who were older and remembered Vittorio, came out of curiosity. A few of these had been patrons in the old days and half hoped to see things as they used to be. They soon realized this wasn't so. Some men had brought their wives and girlfriends which pleased Victoria as it gave the place a real air of respectability.

Luke arrived alone. Victoria knew that Lily couldn't face coming to the building, it held such bad memories for her and although she'd helped Victoria to choose the furnishing for the club, was yet to step inside. However, she'd sent her daughter a huge bouquet of flowers wishing her luck, which brought tears to Victoria's eyes as she read the card.

Good luck, darling. Enjoy tonight as it will never feel quite the same again. Just want to say how proud I am of you and your father would be too. xxx

Victoria loved Luke, her stepfather, who had officially adopted her when he and Lily married. She'd opted to keep her own name in memory of her father and, despite the genuine affection she felt for Luke, there was a deep void in her life that could never be filled. Her father had held her as a baby but she was too young to remember, however hard she tried. She read the card again and hoped Vittorio would have been a proud father.

Luke was very enthusiastic as he was taken on a tour by George Coleman. He hugged Victoria and shook George by the hand. 'My word, you've both done a great job here, the place looks absolutely splendid!'

George invited him to the bar for a drink to celebrate, leaving Victoria to work the room. She talked to all the customers in turn using her natural charm to make them welcome, flattering the ladies, saying she hoped to see them again, answering questions about membership fees and any other queries. She then walked over to the bar towards a young man, tastefully dressed, who stood surveying his surroundings.

'Good evening,' she said, smiling at him. 'You seem to have taken a good look round; do you like what you see?'

He gazed into her eyes, his own twinkling at her as he said, 'Oh yes. Very attractive, very classy.'

It was said with such charm that she had to laugh. Holding out her hand she said, 'Victoria Teglia – and you are?'

He held her hand firmly in his. 'Johnny Daniels at your service. Nice place you have here. Classy, I like that.'

'Are you a local?' she asked, intrigued by him.

'No, Miss Teglia, I'm a Londoner, recently moved here. Expanding my business interests.'

'What kind of business?'

'Construction. During the war, as you can imagine, with the devastation caused by the bombing, I was busy and now I'm able to expand my business here, too.' He handed her a business card:

JOHN DANIELS.
DANIELS CONSTRUCTION INCORPORATED.
5, HIGH STREET. SOUTHAMPTON.

'Like you, my business in the town is new. Here, let me buy you a drink and we can toast success to both of us. What'll it be?'

'Thank you, Mr Daniels, a gin and tonic with ice and lemon.'

George Coleman, standing quietly in the corner of the room, watched the two of them and frowned. He was immediately suspicious of the young shaver and walked over to the bar.

'Mr Daniels here is new to the town, let me introduce you. Mr Daniels, this is George Coleman, we are partners in this business.'

Daniels looked up sharply when he heard the name, but immediately smiled at George. 'Good evening, sir. Nice place you have here.'

'Thanks.' George didn't smile in return. 'So what's your business then?'

Johnny gave him the same spiel as he'd given Victoria.

'Whereabouts in London are you from, son?'

The young man became watchful. 'Camden.'

'I know the area well,' said George, 'don't remember any such construction company there.'

'Ah, that's because we worked near the docks, Camden is where I lived. Can I buy you a drink Mr Coleman?'

George shook his head. 'No thanks, not now. Victoria and I have work to do.'

She took the hint. 'Sorry, have to go, enjoy your evening.' Catching up with George she said, 'You were a bit abrupt weren't you?'

'Something dodgy about that lad, don't know what as yet, but I'll find out if he applies for membership.' And he walked away.

Victoria cast a glance over her shoulder towards the bar, but Johnny Daniels had left.

At that moment, Luke came over to her, kissed her on the cheek and said, 'Sorry, dear, but I have to get back to the hotel, but this all looks an unqualified success. Well done, I'm really proud of you. Let me know if there's anything I can do.'

'Thanks for coming, Luke. Thank Mum for the flowers and tell her all about the club, I know she'll be anxious to know how it went.'

'Don't you worry about that, I've had my instructions. I was to look at everything and give her every detail on my return.'

At midnight, the club closed and the staff sat down with Victoria and George, who opened some champagne for them all to celebrate. Then they discussed how the night had gone in terms of working. Did any of them have any difficulties? Was there enough room between the tables for serving? One or two minor changes were made as a result and then they all went home, tired but elated.

The opening had been a great success and several people had already signed up as members. The bar and restaurant had done a roaring trade and the comments from the customers as they left had been complimentary. Several were also interested in the gambling side, which was an added bonus.

The croupiers had been chosen with care and George had made it very clear that any funny business would be dealt with severely. Aware of his reputation, none of them doubted the threat behind his words. Tonight there had been no gambling, that would only be for members, but the staff had been there for all to see.

Victoria hugged George when at last they were alone. 'Thank you for letting me be a part of this,' she said. 'It was a wonderful night.'

'Couldn't have done it half as well without you, love. Now have a good rest and don't get up too early tomorrow or you'll be out on your feet when we open again.'

As she was driven home in a taxi, Victoria sank back into her seat and closed her eyes. It had all been so exciting and she'd loved every minute. Her thoughts strayed to Johnny Daniels and she smiled. He'd seemed such fun, yet George hadn't shared her opinion and she wondered if he was right about the personable young man. She hoped not.

Two

During the following weeks before Christmas, the Club Valletta was doing well. There had been many applications for membership and, to begin with, those customers who had missed the opening and now came to look the place over were allowed one visit, for which they paid an entrance fee before deciding if it was for them. After that, without membership they would be denied admittance. Before long, the membership list was growing.

A grand formal Christmas Eve celebration for the members and their ladies had been carefully planned. The Club had been tastefully decorated for the festive season and just inside the entrance stood a magnificent Christmas tree, overflowing with baubles and lights. The chef had a celebration menu to offer the customers, to tempt them into the dining room and the croupiers were all dressed as Father Christmas, to add to the jollity.

Johnny Daniels pulled on his dinner jacket, combed his hair and checked out his reflection in the mirror. He grinned broadly. 'How can she resist you, you good-looking devil?' And with a laugh, he placed a white handkerchief in his top pocket and left his flat. As he drove towards the club, he patted his pocket to check he had his membership card with him. He'd not been back to the club since the opening night, but had secured his membership within a few days of his visit. He planned to get to know Miss Victoria Teglia much better before very long.

Johnny walked into the club after showing the vigilant doorman his membership card and made his way to the bar where he ordered a scotch and soda with ice. Glancing around he saw that several of the dining tables were already full and people were still arriving. He'd booked a table for two. He smiled to himself as he saw Victoria greeting her guests. She looked stunning in a long, deep-red evening dress; its well-cut lines showing her neat, curvaceous figure to full advantage.

That cost a pretty penny, he mused, and must have been bought before the wartime utility clothes came into force. He liked a woman with taste as well as spirit and he envisaged an interesting relationship with this young lady, wondering just how long it would take him to get her into bed. He was patient. He'd learned that every woman was different. Some were easily led, others had to be worked on and with her he thought subtlety would be needed. It may take longer but he felt the end result would be well worth the wait.

Unaware of such scrutiny, Victoria was deep in conversation with a group of men who, after they'd had their meal, had come for a night of gambling and Victoria assured them that they had a good choice in the gaming room.

'We try to cater for everyone,' she told them. 'I hope you have a good evening.' And she moved on. As she did so, she glanced over to the bar area and saw Johnny Daniels there. Their gaze met and he smiled and raised his glass at her. She nodded as she turned to greet other customers who had just arrived, getting them seated at their table. She then wandered over to the bar.

'Mr Daniels.'

'Miss Teglia.'

'I see on the reservations you have booked a table for two, is your guest arriving shortly?'

'She's already here,' he said softly.

Victoria looked quickly around. 'In the ladies perhaps?'

'No, standing right beside me looking absolutely wonderful.'

She felt her cheeks flush. 'I don't quite follow you.'

'I was hoping to persuade you to join me for dinner. After all, you must have a break at some time. It would give me so much pleasure if you would accept my invitation.'

For once Victoria was a little flustered. 'Well, I don't quite know what to say.'

'Say yes. It's very simple really.'

She looked at the handsome young man standing before her. There was no doubt that he had infinite charm and was very easy on the eye, but there was something else that drew her to him. There was no menace in his demeanour in any way, but yet there was a hint of danger about him which she found fascinating. She felt he would be hard to handle and, during her time in the navy, she'd had her share of men, but never anyone quite like Johnny Daniels.

'Very well,' she said, 'but I warn you, I can't possibly sit down to dinner until all my customers are settled. After all, they are my first concern.'

'Of course they are, I fully understand that. Business comes first. I'll wait.'

She stared into his eyes searching for some hint of his intentions. They just twinkled back at her, but there was a hint of mischief in his smile. This could be very interesting, she thought.

'I'll see you in a while,' she said as she walked away.

At last everyone was seated, the small band was playing softly so as not to interfere with the conversation of its guests and the chef was busy filling the orders, the waiting staff moving deftly between the tables. Quickly glancing round the room, Victoria walked over to the bar and said to Johnny, who stood in her presence, 'I do believe we can sit down at last. Thank you for waiting.'

'Not at all, after you.'

As they were seated a waiter brought an ice bucket over with a bottle of champagne cooling in it and, given the nod by Johnny, he opened it, filled two glasses and left.

Raising his glass he looked at Victoria. 'To you.'

How very smooth, she thought, and, raising her own glass, drank.

During the meal that followed, Victoria was surprised. She thought her companion would have spent the evening flirting with her, but instead they had the most interesting conversations about his construction work after the Blitz, the odd and sometimes hilarious stories he had to tell. She told him a little of her life in the navy and, before she knew where the time had gone, the meal was finished and she was drinking coffee.

Many of the tables were being vacated by those who wanted to gamble. The more discerning ones who decided not to chance their money stayed and danced.

'Shall we?' asked Johnny looking at the couples already taking to the floor.

Swiftly looking about her to see that everything was running smoothly she looked back at him and said, 'Why not?'

He led her to the centre, took her firmly in his arms and danced her around the floor, to a slow Glenn Miller number.

Victoria could feel the firm frame of her partner as he held her, the scent of his aftershave filled her nostrils and she relaxed in his arms. They didn't speak but moved as if they'd danced together many times before.

George Coleman watched them. Victoria had told him she was having dinner with Johnny Daniels. He hadn't been too enthusiastic, but she'd worked so hard since the club opened and he didn't feel it was his place to argue. After all, what reason could he give her to ask her not to do so? It was just a gut feeling he had, which in the past had never let him down. Now the young man had become a member and would frequently be around, of that he was quite sure. He would make a few discreet enquiries into his background, if only to put his own mind at rest. After all, he felt that Vittorio's daughter was as much his responsibility as her father before her had been.

The gaming room was closed for the final thirty minutes of business and the band stopped the dance music after a final waltz and started to play carols with everyone joining in, singing lustily. It was very fitting as the croupiers, now free, sported red sacks and went around the tables giving small packages to the assembled members and their party. It was an inspired touch to the festivities and greeted with surprise and delight by all.

'Very clever,' Johnny remarked as he took his. 'No doubt this was your idea?'

'What makes you think so?'

He nodded in the direction of the bar where George

Coleman stood like a sentinel, watching the proceedings. 'Your watchdog wouldn't have thought of such a thing in a million years.'

There was a certain tone to his voice that irritated Victoria. 'Mr Coleman is not my watchdog, he's my partner!'

'That, too, I don't doubt, but he looks after you the same way he looked after your father.'

'What do you know about my father?'

The sudden coldness in her voice made Johnny realize he'd made a grave error.

'I didn't know your father, but he's quite a legend around Southampton. After all, he was a hero, so I'm told,' he said quickly, trying to cover his tracks.

But it was too late. Daniels had touched on Victoria's Achilles heel and it was as if she suddenly put a brick wall between them. She rose from her seat.

'Thank you for an enjoyable evening, Mr Daniels,' she said coldly, 'but now I must see to my customers.' She walked away without a backward glance.

Johnny cursed to himself. Whatever had made him say such a thing when the evening, he felt, was going his way and he was beginning to get close to the girl? Now he would have to start all over again, that's if she would let him near her. He paid his bill and left.

As he walked past the bar, George Coleman stepped forward and delayed him.

'You're wasting your time with her son; she's much too smart for the likes of you.'

'I'm not sure what you mean,' Johnny retorted.

'You know exactly what I mean, but I've got your number, you just remember that.'

As Johnny looked into the ice-cold gaze of the man, he knew here was an adversary he would have to watch very carefully.

Christmas Day was spent at the Langford Hotel. Traditionally, Lily, Luke and Victoria served the staff their meals as was the custom before sitting down to join them. Many of the staff members had been at the hotel from the very beginning and there was a definite family feeling around the table as they all tucked in to their turkey and Christmas pudding, pulling crackers and telling stories about the previous years.

George Coleman was of course included in the gathering and Sandy, an old friend of Lily's, had also joined them. He and Lily went back many a year and it had been Sandy who had given her away on her wedding day. Years before, he had been her pianist when she'd been a singer going round the local pubs, trying to earn a living. He'd eventually played piano at the original Club Valletta when Lily had lived there with Vittorio. They shared many a secret. For the past several years he'd lived in London, but they had always kept in touch and Sandy always shared any family celebrations.

Victoria adored him. She loved his outrageous behaviour and sense of humour and he'd watched her grow with a certain pride. They sat together at the table.

During a lull in the conversation Victoria tucked her arm through his. 'So what have you been up to lately, you old devil?'

He feigned indignation. 'Not so much of the old darling *if* you don't mind! Mind you, at sixty I am bloody old, but mentally I'm still thirty-five and dangerous.'

She chuckled. 'You'll never grow old, Sandy, because you've never grown up. How's your love life?'

'You are so cheeky Miss Teglia,' he scolded, then with a sly smile he added, 'actually it's not so bad at the moment. I've met a lovely fellow who's a dancer. A chorus boy I met in a pub a few months ago.'

'Young? How did you manage that?'

'Well, darling, I don't want some old man my age do I? There's no bloody fun in that!'

'Where is he today?'

'With his family as I am with mine. But look.' He held out his wrist and showed her a narrow silver bangle. 'He gave me this last night, sweet boy.'

'And what did you give him?'

'I couldn't possibly tell you, darling!' and he doubled up with laughter.

★   ★   ★

Johnny Daniels was in London with his family, but it couldn't have been more different from the happy scene in Southampton. There was little jollity around this table. Here the conversation was one of money. Big Pat Daniels, Johnny's father, was also in the construction business but it was used as a front. He dealt mainly in stolen goods which were sometimes stored in his large warehouse near the London docks among his building materials. His gang of men were practised house-breakers dealing with homes of the rich and famous, whose movements were often written up in the national papers, giving just the information required by such men. He was advising his son.

'So now you're a member of this exclusive club, you'll be mixing with those who have money. You need to watch the ones who gamble. You'll soon learn to distinguish those who are desperate to make money from those who can afford to lose. I can never understand how the rich so easily part with their money instead of making it work for them.'

'I suppose it depends on how much they have,' Johnny observed.

'And you'll soon see who they are, you just have to watch.'

'It may not be quite as simple as you think, Dad. George Coleman, Vittorio's man, is a partner and he already is suspicious of me.' And he told Pat what George had said to him in the club.

Pat frowned. 'I know about him, he's a hard bastard, but then so was Vittorio Teglia. Full of charm, but cross him and you were really in trouble. The man was ruthless. But there is always a way round a problem, you just have to find it!'

Johnny smiled with some satisfaction. 'I've got that sorted. Victoria Teglia is my way in, Vittorio's daughter. You know I have a way with the ladies, she'll come round in time.'

The older man looked at him through narrowed eyes. 'What if she's a chip off the old block? She may be smarter than you think.'

Young Daniels didn't answer, but he remembered George's words. So she might be clever, but she was also a woman, a woman with needs. He didn't think for one moment she was a virgin, not after serving in the navy. She certainly was not naïve; he was counting on her past experience and he wasn't usually wrong about women.

'I've got some work lined up anyway with a couple of wealthy clients, I'll do a good job for them and soon word will spread and I'll have inside knowledge of the homes and goods of these people, but remember, Dad, you have to give me time to get established. This can't be rushed into.'

'I know that, my son, everything has to be planned. We've always worked that way, and that's why we've been successful. We're bloody careful to cover our tracks.'

And indeed this was the case. The law had yet to catch up with the Danielses although the police had their suspicions; they had never found the evidence needed to convict the criminals.

But as one police chief had said, 'One day they'll make a mistake and we'll be there!'

'Right! That's enough bloody business,' Mrs Daniels protested. 'It's Christmas for God's sake!' And the subject was dropped.

But as he climbed into bed that night, Johnny Daniels made a vow to get Victoria Teglia just where he wanted her, and that was in his bed. Some way or another he was going to succeed.

Three

It was now February and the club was thriving. Victoria and George had opened the dining room at lunch time to accommodate their members who could bring their clients in for lunch and discuss business over a decent meal. They had to be signed into the visitor's book of course, but the gaming room was closed during the day.

Johnny had kept away for several weeks, but occasionally now he brought people in for lunch, greeting Victoria politely, always complimenting her in some way or another, but being careful not to overstep the mark until she became more relaxed and less hostile with him. It was all part of his plan.

His business was taking off, too. To allay any suspicions, he and his father made sure their clients were satisfied with the work done on their houses or factories and they had a good reputation for the legal side of their business and Johnny was getting the same plaudits for his work in Southampton. Some of this filtered back to Victoria through some of her customers and she soon wondered if she'd been somewhat hasty in her attitude towards him. So one evening, when he dropped in for a drink and invited her to join him at the bar, she agreed.

'The club seems to be doing well,' he remarked, as they drank together. 'I'm so pleased for you.'

'Thank you. Yes, George and I are delighted, it has been better than we ever envisaged. And what about you?'

'Me too, there's plenty of business to keep me and my men going for some time in the future, I'm happy to say.' He sighed. 'Mind you, it's the paper work that's the most tedious.'

Laughing she agreed.

'Have you taken a day off since you opened? I bet you haven't!'

Shaking her head she said, 'No. I've not had the time.'

'Neither have I and I feel the need for a break. Why don't we slip off to the New Forest for lunch tomorrow, I think we've earned it? What do you say?'

To her own surprise she agreed. She hadn't meant to say yes, but the word was uttered before she had time to think and when she had done so, she was pleased.

'I'll pick you up at noon and we'll drive to Lyndhurst. Wrap up warm and we'll take a walk to blow the cobwebs away before we eat.'

The following day, Victoria dressed carefully. She wore smart trousers, a sweater and a sheepskin coat. The weather was dry but cold and blustery and she knew that in the New Forest it would be colder. With a certain frisson of excitement she waited at the club after telling George she would be out for most of the day.

He was more than a little surprised to see Johnny Daniels walk into the club and Victoria leave with him and climb into his car. He frowned. This was not good. He'd made enquiries about the young man and, although he only discovered that his business was not only legitimate but well thought of by its clients – a few of them members – he'd also discovered he was the son of Big Pat Daniels and to him, this spelled trouble.

The drive through the New Forest was picturesque. The trees were devoid of leaves at this time of year, but the gorse was flourishing and the New Forest ponies were much in evidence. Had it not been for the many signs asking the public not to feed them, Victoria would have been tempted to stop and do so.

Johnny parked the car and said, 'Come on let's stretch our legs.'

There was an air of peace in the forest and, as they walked, Victoria felt herself unwind. She hadn't realized quite how much the last few months in the new business had taken out of her and after a while she felt renewed.

'I'm really enjoying this,' she said with a look of delight and took his hand as he helped her up a steep incline.

'I'm glad,' he said, keeping hold of her and brushing aside the hair that had fallen over her face in the wind.

At the top of what was a high ridge, they stopped and looked round at the countryside.

'It really is beautiful here at any time of the year,' she remarked, 'but I'm surprised that you liked walking, I wouldn't have thought it was your style at all!'

He started to laugh. 'I'm not quite sure what my "style" is, Victoria, I just felt the need to escape, that's all.'

They walked back to the car and drove to Buckler's Hard and sat in the small inn there where they ate, both ravenous from the exercise. The conversation flowed between them easily and again Victoria was surprised by this young man who was not at all what she expected.

Eventually they drove home and he dropped her outside her flat.

Turning to him in the car she said, 'Thanks, Johnny, that was just what I needed.'

He slipped an arm across her shoulders. 'I'm so pleased. I can't tell you how much I enjoyed your company; perhaps you'll let me take you out again?'

Looking into his eyes that stared back into hers she said, 'Perhaps.'

He drew her slowly towards him and kissed her softly. 'I'll be seeing you,' he whispered as he kissed her again. He then leant across her and opened the door. 'Take care now.'

With a spring in her step, Victoria walked into her lounge and ran her fingers through her tousled hair, looked in the mirror and saw the colour in her cheeks from the wind. Her eyes sparkled. She could still feel the gentle imprint of Johnny's kiss on her mouth and had to admit she'd liked being kissed by him. It had been a very long time since she'd been held in a man's arms and had been surprised by the arousal in her body as he held her. Would she like Johnny Daniels to make love to her? She quickly dismissed the idea. No way was she going to get involved with him, she felt that would be very foolish. But her body told her differently.

That evening, when he got home, Johnny rang his father. 'Things are going just as I planned, Dad. I took Miss Victoria Teglia out to lunch today and we got along just fine.' He listened to the laughter from the man on the end of the line.

Sandy was playing the piano in the Smuggler's Return, in the London docklands – a job he loved – and was paid to appear three nights a week, which gave him some mad money to play with. He was a good pianist and on a Saturday night he gave a turn, singing songs that were popular with a few risqué ones thrown in, to the delight of the patrons who ribbed him unmercifully. He always had an answer and treated the customers – who were mainly villains – with a certain contempt, which they loved. Apart from which, he enjoyed a good gossip and this pub was aptly named as the customers were mainly members of the underworld. Notorious villains who knew they were in a pub which catered for their ilk. The landlord was an old lag and had served time himself. His wife held the licence but he was the boss and everybody knew that and, as he was a hard man, they treated him with a respect that he'd earned over the years.

Big Pat Daniels and his gang had made the Smuggler's Return their local. Other factions of London's various gangs knew better than to encroach on his patch. He was definitely the Lord of the Manor in these parts and you had better respect that unless you wanted real trouble. And it was here, on occasion, that Johnny met with his father.

Sandy liked Johnny. He had more polish than his father. He had style, which endeared him to the old pianist who loved to see a man well turned out. What's more, he treated Sandy with respect, sadly lacking among the others, who, although he amused them, did like to ridicule him whenever they could, even if it was done humorously. But never Johnny. Sandy had always thought that, if the lad had had a different father, he could go a long way in the legitimate world. He was intelligent and had great charm.

When on this particular evening Johnny walked into the bar, Sandy winked at him and nodded to where Pat was sitting. He was playing quietly and could hear the voices raised above the hub bub of the crowd. He pricked up his ears when he heard the name Victoria on young Johnny's lips.

'She's a lovely girl, Dad, I really like her.'

Pat glowered at his son. 'Don't start getting fond of her son, she's a means to an end and don't you forget it! It starts getting personal, it won't work.'

Sandy was worried. It had to be his Victoria because he knew that Johnny was a member of the club as George Coleman had had a quiet word with him when he'd discovered Pat Daniels was the father, knowing that Sandy played piano in Pat's London local. What was going on? He needed to find out. He continued to listen but the conversation changed to other things.

A little later, Johnny wandered over with a half of bitter for the pianist as was his habit. 'Here you are, Sandy. How are you doing?'

'Fine thanks love, and you? How's business?' It was no secret that Johnny had started up in Southampton and he'd heard that's where Sandy came from and in the past they had talked about the town.

'Doing well, thanks, Sandy.'

'Found yourself a good woman yet?' It was a well-known fact that the good-looking young man had a way with women and Sandy had often teased him about it in the past.

Johnny laughed. 'As a matter of fact I have but the trouble is she *is* a good woman! I like them better when they're naughty.'

'Oh my, tell me more . . . could it be you've met your match?'

'We'll have to wait and see,' was the answer and Johnny walked away. Leaving Sandy none the wiser.

It was mid-morning a few days later and Victoria was checking out the dining-room tables in readiness for the lunchtime trade, when a familiar voice made her turn round.

'Hello, tiger, you still look good enough to eat!'

'Bruce!' She rushed into the arms of a good-looking naval officer who lifted her off her feet, swung her round before kissing her until she was breathless.

'Bloody hell, Victoria, you have no idea how I've missed you!'

'You were at sea when I came home, there was no way I could say goodbye except to send you a signal. You look wonderful.' And she kissed him again.

'Why didn't you write to me?' he demanded.

'Well, after my demob, I got caught up in this.' She gestured to the room. 'I'm a partner in this business!'

'I know, I went to the Langford Hotel and your mother told me where you were.' He raised his eyebrows as he questioned her. 'How could you just walk out on me like that after all we'd been to each other?'

'I'm sorry, darling. There was so much to do before we opened. This used to be my father's club in the old days you know . . . Well, not as you see it now, it's been rebuilt a couple of times. Come and let me show you round.' And she took him on a tour, introducing him to George Coleman as she went.

George was delighted to meet him as it was obvious to everyone that these two were very close. Thank God, he thought, now she'll have someone else to think about other than bloody Johnny Daniels.

Eventually the couple sat at the bar and over a drink caught up with each other's news. Captain Bruce Chapman held her hand as they talked. 'God I've missed you, darling,' he said.

'I'm on leave for two weeks. I do hope we'll be able to spend some time together.'

Victoria gazed into his eyes and realized just how much this man meant to her. They'd had a torrid affair during their time together. At first it had been based on lust but it had grown into more than that by the time she left the navy and she had meant to write to him, but with one thing and another, their relationship had been pushed to the back of her mind and now she felt guilty about it. Bruce didn't deserve to be treated so lightly but now she'd make it up to him.

'Let's go to The Langford and have some lunch, then you can meet the family. After, we'll go home.'

'When you say home, where do you mean?'

She caressed his cheek. 'My flat.'

He grinned broadly. 'I like the sound of that. Do we need to eat first?'

With a chuckle she said, 'I'm afraid so, I promised them. I try and lunch with Mum and Luke as often as possible.'

'Then I'll try to contain myself until later,' he said, teasing.

Victoria felt very proud as she walked into her parents' establishment. Bruce looked so smart in his uniform with his gold braid and medal ribbons on his chest. He'd survived many dramas during the war and had been torpedoed once and now he was captain of his own vessel. He was tall with blonde hair and had an air of command about him which certainly seemed to impress the receptionist who couldn't take her eyes off him as they waited for Lily and Luke to join them.

The lunch was an enjoyable time, the two men hit it off immediately and Lily, listening to them chat, turned to her daughter.

'How come you've never told me about Bruce? He's wonderful, just the sort of man I hoped you would marry.'

'Steady, Mum. Nothing has been mentioned about marriage, we're just friends, that's all.'

Lily gave a sardonic smile. 'Rather more than that I think, Victoria.'

★   ★   ★

This the two of them proved when they entered the door of Victoria's flat and Bruce took her into his arms. 'You still look amazing and I can't wait to make love to you again,' he said softly as he nuzzled her neck.

The familiarity of the man who held her, and kissed her, brought forth the old longings and she led him into her bedroom. 'Show me,' she said as she started to undress.

Bruce knew her and her needs so well, he knew exactly which buttons to press and their love making was long and languid as he explored her body with his long fingers and his tongue until she was all but frantic for him to take her. And when eventually he entered her, her soft cries of ecstasy pleased him, knowing that he was giving her pleasure.

Eventually they lay together curled in each other's arms. 'My God, how I've missed that,' he said.

'You mean you've been celibate?' she asked.

He looked surprised. 'Of course, what a strange question. You know how much I think of you, why would I want anyone else?'

'It's been a long time, Bruce.'

'A bloody long time! I felt like a monk . . . and you?'

She immediately thought of Johnny Daniels kissing her. 'Me too.' It wasn't a lie; a kiss didn't mean anything after all.

'I'm being stationed in Portsmouth after my leave,' he told her.

'Oh, Bruce, that's marvellous!'

'I'm so pleased you sound so happy about it, darling. You know, after so long, I did wonder if you felt the same as me. The navy is my career, as you know, there will be times when I'm away, how do you feel about that?'

'What are you trying to say?'

He turned her in his arms so he could look at her. 'I'm saying that I missed you like hell and would like to think we could be together permanently.'

Four

Victoria was stunned by Bruce's words and didn't know what to say. The pregnant pause made him frown.

'What's the matter, I thought you loved me – well you used to, at least that's what you told me when we were together.'

'Oh Bruce, I do, truly. You've just knocked the wind out of my sails, that's all. It's been so long since last we met. Today you walked back into my life and it was wonderful to see you – but marriage?'

'What's so wrong with marriage?' he demanded.

'Nothing, nothing at all, I suppose it was never on my agenda, the business has been my only concern for months.'

'Obviously!' He sounded cross. 'Otherwise you would have written to me.'

She cuddled into him. 'Don't be mad with me, Bruce, not just after we've made love, it'll spoil the moment.'

He let out a deep sigh. 'Oh, Victoria, what am I going to do about you?'

'You could love me some more.'

'Are you turning me down?' he persisted.

'No, darling, but let's just get used to being together again. You'll be around if you're going to be based in Portsmouth – let's leave it at that for now.'

'But you will think about it?'

'Of course I will – but don't pressure me, Bruce. There's no mad rush after all.'

He took her into his arms and softly kissed her. He would have to be patient, he could see that. Victoria was only just beginning to settle down to civilian life, which was never easy and she had started a new business. Perhaps he was a bit previous, but he wanted her as his wife, the mother of his children. They were good together and he was sure he could make her happy. Then he was besieged by doubts. Perhaps she'd met someone else after all? Well, he'd be around for the next while and that would have to be enough for now.

During the rest of the week, Victoria spent as much time as she could with Bruce, trying to make up for the past, but on Saturday night she told him she'd have to work.

'Come to the club and when everything is running well, we'll have dinner.' And he'd agreed.

This particular Saturday, the club was heaving with people and Victoria was busy looking after the welfare of her customers. Bruce sat at the bar watching her work the room, admiring her expertise with people. She worked hard and he felt a certain pride at her achievements.

It was whilst he went to the gents that Johnny Daniels walked in. He made for the bar, sat on a high stool and ordered a drink. Greeting one or two members who were now his clients.

Victoria wandered over and had a word with him. 'Hello, Johnny, how are you?'

Casually putting an arm round her waist he said, 'Fine. My goodness you're busy tonight. Too busy to have dinner with me?'

'Sorry, Johnny, I'm already booked.' She made her excuses and went to greet some members who had just arrived. He took little notice of the naval officer who sat near him at the bar, but soon wandered into the gaming room to watch the players, to see who could afford to lose their money without becoming upset over their losses. After all, that's what he was here for.

One roulette table was playing to high rollers and he stood and watched. It was quite obvious to the casual observer that several of the men were seasoned gamblers, placing their chips with alacrity, but one man in particular was losing heavily and Johnny watched the man wipe the sweat from his brow as he lost his chips once again, whereas the others collected their winnings with much jollity and banter.

The loser asked for an extended line of credit and the croupier said he'd have to ask his boss. George Coleman was summoned. The croupier whispered in his ear and George glanced over to the unlucky punter, then walked around the table, took the man firmly by the elbow, said something quietly and waited.

The man started to argue. Towering over him, George's demeanour became threatening, but he kept his voice low, uttered a few words which made the man pale, then he led him away.

Curious, Johnny walked to the door of the room and watched as George took the man to the entrance. He heard what was said.

'You have seven days to pay your debts or I'll be making a personal call on you,' he said, threateningly. 'And believe me, you wouldn't enjoy that.'

Johnny slipped back into the gaming room. George Coleman was certainly not to be messed with. He casually asked one of the passing waiters the names of the other men who had been winning at the table, then walked back into the dining area and the bar. He looked around for Victoria and was surprised to see her dining with the naval officer. He sat and watched them and was not pleased. The man sitting with Victoria reached across the table and took her hand. It was the way she looked back at him that displeased Johnny so much. He beckoned the barman over.

'Who is that with Miss Teglia?'

'Captain Chapman, I believe he's an old friend she knew when she was in the WRNS.'

George Coleman saw the way Johnny Daniels was watching Victoria and chuckled to himself. 'Now that's a real man, my son,' he muttered to himself. 'You've got no chance.'

But he had no idea how persistent the young man could be when he had something – or someone – in his sights. Johnny Daniels didn't like losing.

During the following week, Daniels made discreet enquiries about the men who'd been gambling at the Club Valletta and discovered they were indeed wealthy. One had a large impressive residence in nearby Romsey, another lived in Basset – a very salubrious area – and the third was a minor member of the aristocracy. All of whom had priceless antiques in their homes and the latter was a collector of fine art. He'd hit pay dirt, as the Americans would say. His father would be delighted with this knowledge. Johnny would leave the rest to him. He had to make sure he was beyond reproach with an unbreakable alibi for the times the burglaries would take place. He would go up to London this weekend and pass on the information to Pat.

It was Saturday night at The Smugglers Return and Sandy was doing his piece when Johnny arrived. The young man walked quietly to the bar and ordered a drink as he listened to the pianist perform.

Sandy was on form this night and the laughter filled the bar as he sang a song full of double entendres. Johnny laughed along with the others and when Sandy had finished he took him over the usual half of beer.

'You were very naughty tonight, you old queen,' he said, joking.

'Well you know what Mae West says, "When I'm good I'm very, very good, but when I'm bad, I'm better!"'

Laughing, Johnny said, 'You'll never go to heaven when you die.'

'No, darling, I'll go below with all my friends . . . might meet your old man there!'

Johnny walked away shaking his head at the man's audacity and sat beside his father. From his pocket he took out an envelope.

'Here you are, Dad, a list of very likely clients.' And he proceeded to tell him what he'd discovered.

'Well done, son! I'll go through this and then I'll send a couple of my men down to Southampton to check out the houses. I'll let you know when it's going down so you can be in evidence somewhere. Right?'

'Give me as much notice as you can so I've time to make my own plans.'

'How you getting on with the Teglia girl?' asked Pat.

'She's tied up with some flashy naval officer at the moment, but I can wait. He's probably on leave and that can't last for ever. Then I'll move in on her.'

'You be careful.'

Sandy, sitting at his piano watched the scene between father and son, but tonight there was no way he could hear what they were saying, there was too much noise and he was too far away. But he'd seen Johnny hand over an envelope and would have given his right arm to have known the contents.

The following day, Pat talked to three of his trusted criminals and told him of his plan.

'Take yourself down to Southampton, find a cheap bed and breakfast and check out these houses. Find out as much as you can about the residents, how many in the household, when they go out and, whenever possible, get inside and take a look around. We need to know what's there. Be careful, we don't want the punters to know you've been inside. You know what to do.'

These men were practised at their work; they'd been at it for years. No house was impregnable to them. They knew exactly what to look for and were very knowledgeable about antiques and their worth. Sometimes, when the house was not empty during the time they had to check it out, they would knock on the door quite blatantly, pretending to check the phone line or look for a gas leak. Residents were gullible and once they flashed an official-looking card at them, were never refused entrance and so they set off to do the groundwork for their boss.

It was the last day of Bruce's leave and he'd taken Victoria to Bournemouth.

During the two weeks of his leave, they had regained the intimacy of their relationship and, as they dined, Bruce caught hold of her hand.

'I've so enjoyed being with you again, darling, and thank God I'm going to be around, I can't bear the idea of us being parted again.'

Victoria said softly. 'It's been great. I didn't realize how much I'd missed you, but you do realize, Bruce, that I may not always be free when you are. The club is still very new and I've got to continue to work hard to make it a success.'

'I do understand, Victoria, and you deserve to do well, you work so hard and you're good at what you do. But remember, you must take some time to smell the daisies. You have to have a life after all.'

She squeezed his hand and chuckled. 'Listen if you were around too long all the time, I wouldn't have the energy to work!'

He burst out laughing. 'Having sex is great exercise, it keeps you fit!'

'Fit for nothing with your appetite!'

'Listen, I had a lot of catching up to do, if you will leave me alone for so long you have to pay the price.'

'You, Captain Chapman, are insatiable!'

'You can sleep on the train on the way home. After all, tonight is my last night with you and I don't know when next I'll be free.'

The following evening, when Johnny Daniels entered the club, he was delighted to find Victoria on her own and when she walked over to greet him he questioned her.

'No handsome naval escort tonight?'

'No, his leave is over. Why?'

'I've missed talking to you, that's all. I didn't want to encroach on another man's patch.' His eyes twinkled mischievously as he looked at her.

'I wouldn't have thought that would have made any difference to you, frankly!'

He had to laugh because she was absolutely right. Normally he'd still have stepped in, but with her he was treading carefully. 'Would you have objected if I had?'

He was flirting outrageously with her and she knew it, but there was something about this man that could not be denied. She got a certain pleasure out of playing his game.

'I might not have but my friend wouldn't have been too pleased.'

'Had I been in his place I would be furious,' he said. 'But sadly I was not and that is my loss.'

'You have such a silver tongue, Mr Daniels. I bet you've left a trail of broken hearts behind you.'

He grinned at her. 'A few.'

'Well, you won't break mine!'

He caressed her cheek. 'I would never do that to you,' he said, with great sincerity.

Cocking her head on one side she looked at him. 'You sounded as if you really meant that. You are a dangerous man to know, I think.'

'Why don't you try and get to know me better and find out?'

'That might be interesting, Johnny, but I have a club to run and don't really have the time.'

'You know you don't really mean that. From the very first moment we met there has been a chemistry between us, I know it, and if only you would be honest with yourself, you know it too.' His steady gaze never left hers.

Staring back at him, Victoria knew he spoke the truth. Whatever it was between them, this man drew her like a moth to the flame and she knew that eventually she would go out with him again.

'I have to work,' she said.

'I can wait, Victoria, because I know in the end it will be worthwhile.' He leaned forward and brushed her lips lightly with his, then he got off the bar stool and left the club.

She watched him walk away, willing him to turn round . . . but he didn't.

Five

Lily was waiting at the railway station for the train from Waterloo to arrive. Sandy had called her two days ago and said he wanted to see her and she wondered what was the reason behind his visit. Whatever it was, she would be delighted to spend a few hours with her old and trusted friend, and when he emerged from the exit and climbed into her car, she kissed his cheek.

'Hello, you old tart, where do you want to go?'

'You'll think I'm mad but let's go to the pier, sit in a deck chair and eat fish and chips out of a paper.'

'Oh, Sandy, that would be great! It's been a few years since we last did that together and then only if the punters had been generous after I'd sung and you went round the bar with the hat.'

'Don't you even forget those days, darling, they made you into the person you are now. You know what hard grind is and therefore you appreciate the good things in life.'

A little later, both Lily and Sandy were huddled together in deckchairs in a sheltered spot, tucking into fish and chips wrapped in newspaper. Fortunately the day was dry but, in early March, the sea breeze was cool to say the least. But the two of them ignored it as they ate and chatted. When eventually they had finished, Lily collected all the paper and deposited it in a waste bin, then came back and sat down.

'Now, Sandy, what's on your mind?'

'It's young Victoria as a matter of fact.'

Lily frowned. 'Victoria?' She gazed at her friend, puzzled by his remark.

'She's getting involved with a young geezer called Johnny Daniels, son of a major London gangster who uses the pub that I play in at weekends and I heard a whisper, that's all.'

'How involved *is* she? Only, she's been seeing a naval captain who seems not only an old friend but a lover, too, and from what I've seen Victoria was pretty smitten.'

'That's as might be, Lily, but young Johnny is a very charming young man and I do believe he's keen on her. I just don't want her to become involved with the low life as her father was, that's all.'

'Right, I'll have a word with George Coleman and see what's going on, thanks, Sandy. I never go to the club, as you know.'

'Maybe you should, Lily, and see this young man for yourself before anything happens and it's too late to stop it. You're a pretty shrewd judge of character, look him over. I know it won't be easy for you, after all, that's where Vittorio died, but try and remember the good times there. I wouldn't ask this of you, but frankly I'm worried.'

'Victoria is far more important than my feelings, Sandy. I'll talk to George, find out when this man will be there and I'll do as you ask. I promise. Come on, let's live it up and have a pot of tea at the cafe and then I'll drive you back to the station.'

As she drove home, Lily pondered over Sandy's words. It was her one fear that somehow Victoria might be drawn back into the criminal world like Vittorio and, with the club retaining its name, she always felt that one day this would happen. Well, she would put a stop to it, one way or another.

Later that evening, Lily rang the Club Valletta and asked to speak to Coleman. He confirmed what Sandy had told her and she arranged to meet him the following morning at the hotel, where he could give her all his information. She replaced the receiver and sighed. It was as she had predicted, the worms had started crawling out of the woodwork. Well, if she had anything to do with it, they could crawl right back again! Victoria would not be plagued by them; she wanted her to have a good life, unsullied by the sort of men she had had to deal with in hers. Hopefully Victoria would settle with Bruce, the naval officer. He looked man enough to cope with her wilful daughter.

The following morning, George Coleman arrived at the Langford Hotel and was shown into Lily's private sitting room, where she sent for a pot of coffee.

'Now tell me about this young man Sandy was talking about.'

'He's good looking, well dressed, oozes charm and to be honest is very personable, but in my gut I felt from the beginning he was dodgy. When he became a member I did some digging. His old man, Big Pat Daniels, is a big London villain. He and the boy are in the construction business, all legal and above board, very professional and some of our members speak highly of his work.' He rubbed his nose thoughtfully. 'So far so good but . . .'

'But what?' Lily urged.

'Two things, girl. He's got some other reason for being a member. Let's face it, lots of the clients are wealthy, from the top drawer. Victoria set out to get the best and she succeeded. What better set of victims for a criminal element? Apart from which, he's taken a shine to Victoria.'

Lily sipped her coffee as she collected her thoughts. 'But what about Captain Chapman? I thought he and Victoria were pretty close.'

'Ah, the naval chappie. Now there is a real man, our girl could do far worse. But you know Lily; this young Johnny Daniels has a way with the ladies, that much I've learned. He's cut quite a swathe across the female population in London.'

'Mmm. I've met his type but then I expect so has Victoria. After all she's been in the navy for long enough to know about men.'

He chuckled. 'You should know, darlin', that the dangerous ones are the most attractive.'

She smiled to herself as she remembered. How often had she been warned against Vittorio? But he had such charisma. He was also dangerous to know and that had added to the attraction, but she had been lucky. He'd treated her well, given her a child and eventually she had fallen in love with him . . . and then sadly he'd died. But not all men were like him. The criminal element were hard and could snuff out a life if it got in the way without compunction – and that was even more of a worry. No, she would have to see for herself.

'When he next comes into the club, call me. I want to meet him.'

George knew what it would cost Lily to walk through the doors of the club and his admiration for her grew even more. She had been through so much during the years he'd known her and she'd never shirked when it came to facing her demons.

He rose from his seat. 'I'll do that. It's usually at the weekend. You know, don't you, that as long as I draw breath, that girl will be safe.'

'I know, George, and I'll always be grateful – you know that too.'

The following Saturday evening, Johnny Daniels entered the club and took his usual place at the bar. It was early and he hoped he'd be able to chat up Victoria before she got too involved with her customers. He'd decided to move in on her. The naval captain was off the scene and now was his chance to begin to cement a relationship that he was really looking forward to. And he was lucky; as he ordered his drink, Victoria emerged from the kitchen and, seeing Johnny, walked over to him.

'You're in here early.'

'Thought we might have a quiet drink together before the rush, that's all. What will you have?'

'Just a tonic water, please, I've got a long night ahead.'

Whilst they were talking, George rang the Langford Hotel and informed Lily of the young man's arrival. Then he waited.

Johnny was regaling Victoria with some story that she obviously found amusing and, as she was sitting with her back to the entrance, was unaware that her mother had entered the premises until she felt a hand on her shoulder.

'Hello, darling, thought it was time I came to see what you'd done to the old place.' She nodded at Johnny. 'Good evening, I don't think we've met . . .'

For a moment Victoria was speechless. 'Oh, oh . . . sorry. Johnny, this is my mother, Mrs Langford. This is Johnny Daniels, one of our members.'

He held out his hand. 'How do you do? I've seen you in your hotel, can I get you a drink?'

'Thank you, but not at the moment, I want to look around but after would be nice.' Turning to her daughter she said, 'How about a guided tour?'

Victoria climbed down from the bar stool and took Lily's hand. 'I never thought you'd come here, but I'm so very happy that you did.' She was delighted. 'I so wanted you to see what we've done, George and me. Come on.'

With great enthusiasm she showed her mother over the establishment, room by room, introducing her to the chef and the other staff. All of them were slightly in awe of this elegant, sophisticated woman, with an air about her. Then they returned to the bar.

'Now, Mr Daniels, I would like a gin and tonic with ice and lemon, thank you.' Lily informed him as she sat on the stool beside him.

Johnny nodded to the barman who stood waiting. 'What about you, Victoria?' But at that moment she was called away, leaving him and Lily alone.

'So, Mr Daniels, as a member, what are your impressions of this establishment?'

'It's well run, the staff are very efficient, the ambience is lovely, the clientele are quality, which is down to your daughter – who is wonderful with people. I'm sure she'll be a huge success.'

Lily sipped her drink as she listened. Yes, she could see the attraction here. Johnny Daniels was well groomed, good mannered, personable . . . and quite fascinating to a young woman. He was smooth, far too smooth, and she knew immediately why George Coleman was worried. This was a younger version of Vittorio, but did he have the good qualities that made Vittorio different from other villains?

'What line of business are you in, if I may ask?'

'Construction. I've done quite a lot of business for several of the members here.'

She raised her eyebrows. 'So it's a good hunting ground for you?'

There was something in her voice as she made this remark that put Johnny on his guard. This woman was smart, he knew she'd been the mistress of The Maltese and therefore was not unfamiliar with the seamy side of life, the life he'd been born into, and he knew he'd have to watch his step.

'Well, Mrs Langford, you are a shrewd business woman so you'll understand that it's often not what you know but who you know that helps you succeed in the world of business.'

'Absolutely! But of course to build a good reputation, you have to have one. Do you have one, Mr Daniels?'

Was she mocking him? He wasn't quite sure how to handle this woman and that was a first for him. 'I certainly hope so, Mrs Langford.'

'So do I, because I believe you have an interest in my daughter. Therefore, I have an interest in you. Victoria is very precious to me and if I thought you might hurt her in any way at all, I would be more than a little displeased.'

Johnny realized by the steel in her voice that this was no idle threat. Lily Langford was throwing down the gauntlet to him and he had better be careful how he answered.

'It would be the last thing I would do. I admire Victoria; she's a wonderful girl, why would I want to hurt her?'

'I can't imagine and let's hope I don't have to ask myself that question in the future.'

At that moment Victoria returned and Lily climbed off the bar stool and kissed her on the cheek. 'I have to fly, darling. After all, I have a business of my own to run. You've done a wonderful job here and I'm very proud of you.' She turned to Johnny. 'It was nice meeting you Mr Daniels.' She gave him a piercing look. 'You take care now.' And she walked to the door with her daughter.

George Coleman watched her leave with a knowing look. He'd seen her talking to young Daniels and recognized the expression on her face. She was telling him the score, of that he was certain, and from the look on the boy's face, he'd got the message. Job well done, Lily.

When Victoria returned she asked, 'What did you think of my mother, isn't she wonderful?'

'Indeed she is. A formidable woman I would say.'

Victoria laughed, then made her excuses as her clients started arriving.

Johnny sat quietly drinking, going over his conversation with Victoria's mother. He glanced over to where Coleman was talking to a man and wondered just how much he'd had to do with this visit tonight? And . . . if he was to upset the apple cart, would it be Coleman who would be sent to sort him out? He didn't doubt that it would be, but there was an even bigger worry. If his father was setting up his gang to burgle some of the houses belonging to the wealthy members of the club, would the trail eventually lead back to him? Now he began to worry.

Six

The following Wednesday evening, Sandy was in the Smuggler's Return, having a quiet drink and chat with the barman before the evening began, when the door opened and Johnny Daniels walked in. Sandy looked at him with interest.

'Evening, young man, a little out of your way aren't you, so early in the week?'

'Just thought I'd pop in and have a drink with Dad, he said he'd be in later.'

He seemed to be a little agitated, which was very unusual, and Sandy wondered if Lily had anything to do with this.

'So how's things, young shaver? Still keeping busy?'

'Yes, thanks, Sandy, the business is picking up well. I made the right move going to Southampton, I'm happy to say.'

'And how's your love life and that *good* girl you were telling me you'd met?'

The young man relaxed a little. 'I don't have a love life at the moment, I'm sad to say.'

'Am I hearing right?' Sandy pretended to be shocked. 'What about the girl, blow you out did she?'

Johnny's ego wouldn't let this pass. 'No, as a matter of fact she hasn't and later this week I'm going to ask her out.'

At that moment, Pat Daniels entered the bar with a couple of his henchmen and Sandy took his leave and made his way to the piano where he started playing very quietly, his gaze never leaving the men as they settled nearby at a table.

He couldn't hear what was being said, but tried to guess by the change of expressions on the faces of father and son as they talked. He'd have been more than interested had he been able to overhear the conversation.

'Well, son, what's so important that couldn't wait?'

'It's the jobs your men have been casing; I want you to call them off.'

'You mad or what?'

'No, Dad, I'm serious, we've got to put them on hold for a while.'

Pat snorted with derision. 'Give me one good reason!'

'Lily Langford, Victoria's mother came into the club last Saturday. She warned me off her daughter.'

His father roared with laughter which made Sandy sit up very quickly.

'Is that all? Your love life's got nothing to do with the business.'

Johnny persisted. 'This time it has! It was the way she spoke to me implying without saying anything as if she was on to me.'

'You're not making any sense, my son.'

Johnny shook his head in frustration. 'All I know is if you pull a job too soon, she'll put two and two together and I'll be finished down there. She smells a rat, I could tell, and remember, Dad, she lived with The Maltese, so she's no fool!'

Pat stared long and hard at his son as he pondered his words. 'All right, my boy, I'll take all that on board. But I want you to do me a favour next Monday.'

'What's that?'

'I've got a shipment of iron girders arriving at the docks and I want you to go down and check them in. I'll give you the manifest. They're coming from Holland and I don't trust those Dutch buggers so I want you personally to see to it for me.'

'Yes, of course. Have you got the papers with you?'

The two men pored over the documents together. 'The ship docks at ten thirty in the morning,' said Pat. 'You be there when it arrives and don't leave until everything is clear and the papers signed. All right, got that?'

'Yes, Dad, don't worry, I'll see to it.' Finishing his drink, Johnny rose from his seat and left the bar, winking at Sandy on the way out.

As the pianist's fingers covered the keys, he wondered just what had passed between father and son. Johnny had been unusually serious and the old man looked as if he was mulling things over in his mind before he spoke. Something was going down, of that he was sure.

One of Pat's men who had been listening to the conversation spoke. 'So that's put the mockers on our plans then, guv?'

'Don't be a bloody fool! The timing couldn't be better. We may not get such a good chance again and now Johnny will be out of the way in full view of the dock police – and the customs – what stronger alibi could he have? No we go.'

At the Langford Hotel, Luke and Lily were in conference with the chef. Since last month, a world food shortage brought about the return to food rationing on a near-wartime basis and the chef had no choice but to scale down the menu. Much of their stuff was purchased from local farmers. The chickens, local pork and, when they could, a side of beef. Vegetables were not a problem; the market gardeners grew their own and supplied the hotel. But the cereals for poultry and animal consumption were being drastically reduced. The chef wasn't happy.

'We beat the bloody Jerries in the war and now we have to feed the bleeders,' he stormed. 'Let the buggers starve I say!'

Lily tried to placate him. 'All their agricultural industry has been destroyed, chef, and we did that to them.'

'Excuse me, madam, but had it been the other way round, would they care about us? Would they hell!'

Luke intervened. 'You're probably right, chef, but the fact is we have to simplify the choices on the menu.'

'As a matter of fact, sir, I've pulled a few strokes which I'd rather keep to myself if you don't mind. I can get the poultry we need, well, most of it, and I've managed to put some pork in the freezer and—'

Luke stopped him. 'Don't tell me any more, we'll leave it to you to do the best you can.'

'Thank you, sir, I promise our reputation won't suffer, you have my word.'

As the two of them left the kitchen, Luke chuckled. 'That man is worth a fortune to us, Lily. I only hope he knows what he's doing.'

Tucking her arm through his she laughed. 'He's far too smart to get caught doing whatever he's up to. Come on, let's take a quick walk round the park and get some fresh air before we start.'

After a while, they sat on a bench, people watching until Luke spoke.

'When are you going to tell me why you took yourself off to the Club Valletta the other day, Lily?'

She looked at him with surprise.

'I heard you tell the receptionist where you would be if you were needed, yet you didn't mention it to me and I wondered why?'

She paused, wondering just how much to disclose to her

husband. If he knew about Johnny Daniels and his background, he would worry, and at this stage she decided it unnecessary to share her concerns.

'I thought I was being selfish not seeing the effort that Victoria and George had put into their business. After all, the past is the past . . . and I'm pleased I did go. You were right; they've done a grand job.'

Luke wasn't fully convinced as he looked at her, but if Lily had another reason, no doubt she would tell him in time. He'd learned over the years that his wife was very much her own woman and, indeed, that had been part of her attraction. He would just have to trust her.

The following Monday, Johnny Daniels made his way to the docks to check on the shipment of iron girders for his father, as promised. He walked into the customs shed and produced the necessary documents, had a chat with the officer and waited for the shipment to be unloaded. It took some time and eventually, several hours later, he handed over papers at the dock gates to the police on duty and sat beside the driver of the lorry moving the load, and left the docks behind.

Meanwhile, the house in Chilworth belonging to The Honourable Henry Charterhouse was being burgled. Henry was away, staying with relatives in The Cotswolds, unaware that the alarm, fitted at great expense, had been expertly dismantled by professionals.

Pat Daniels' men had done their homework very thoroughly. Under the guise of security men from the company that had installed the alarm, they had arrived a few days previously, to give the system an overhaul. Armed with false papers and dressed in the appropriate uniforms, they had easily gained access to the house without arousing the suspicions of the housekeeper. Now they collected a small painting by Goya and two first editions from the library, all going to private collectors who would pay a high price to own them and keep them in a private room for their own pleasure, without enquiring from whence they came, only thrilled to have them as part of their collection.

The housekeeper was out shopping as was her habit every

Monday morning and Henry's valet had travelled with his employer, and so the intruders had an easy time. They were in and out of the house in minutes, resetting the alarm before they left.

It was days before the housekeeper noticed the empty space on the drawing-room wall and reported the loss to the police after informing her employer, who came rushing back from his holiday where he also discovered the loss of the books.

It was the main topic of conversation in the Club Valletta, after the news made the front page of the *Southern Daily Echo*.

George Coleman read the report and frowned.

When Johnny Daniels saw the headlines he was livid. His father had completely ignored his warning. Now he knew why he'd been sent to the docks: so that he had an airtight alibi. It hadn't taken the police very long to realize when the burglary had taken place as the Monday morning was the only time the house had been empty. Johnny was thankful that Henry Charterhouse hadn't been one of his clients; that would have given him cause to worry. As it was, he wondered if George Coleman and, indeed, Lily Langford would put two and two together. He would just have to bluff it out. He would go to the club that evening or it might seem suspicious if he kept away.

Later that evening, Johnny took a deep breath as he walked through the door of Club Valletta, knowing his actions would be carefully scrutinized by Victoria's watchdog. He sat at the bar as was his habit and ordered a beer.

'Read about Mr Charterhouse's house being done?' the barman asked as he poured the drink.

'Yes, saw it in tonight's paper. How awful for him.'

'Can't understand it. It said in the paper the alarm was working, the police tried it.' He placed the full glass in front of Johnny. 'I suppose he was insured but still, knowing some-one's been in your house uninvited is a bit of a worry. You could be murdered in your bed!' He walked away to serve another customer.

'Don't suppose you know anything about it do you, Daniels?'

Johnny turned to find George Coleman beside him.

'Me? Why would I know anything?'

Coleman glared at him, his eyes piercing and cold. 'Because I reckon your old man's behind it and you fed him the information, that's why!'

Johnny felt his heart racing, but he held the other's gaze. 'That's a serious allegation, Mr Coleman, and one I take exception to, frankly.'

George leaned closer until Johnny could feel the man's breath as he spoke. 'Now you listen and listen good. If I find out you or your family – through you – have anything to do with this, you won't make old bones, my boy, and that's no idle threat, it's a promise.'

'You're barking up the wrong tree.' The young man protested. 'Why would I jeopardize my good reputation when my business is doing so well? It would be madness. Of course I had nothing to do with it. My dad and I are in the construction business, that's all.'

'Now you're underestimating my intelligence, boy! I know your old man of old, so don't try and make him out to be a bloody saint, not to me.'

'I am *not* my father!' Johnny protested, his face flushed with anger.

'Maybe, but the acorns don't fall far from the tree.'

As George walked away, Johnny Daniels took a swig from his beer. He could feel the beads of perspiration on his brow but didn't dare wipe them away. He'd kill his father for putting him in this situation.

Whilst his son was fuming in Southampton, Pat Daniels was counting his money. The painting was safely out of the country, before its loss had been discovered, packaged among the painting materials and landscapes of an elderly woman off on a painting holiday to France where it had been delivered to its buyer. The books were now part of a private library in a castle in the north of Scotland.

Pat knew that his son would be angry with him, but business was business. However, he would now wait a good while before he pulled another job in Southampton. No good getting greedy. Perfect timing was one of his strong points. He could wait. There were other jobs on hand anyway and he had plenty of construction work to keep him busy meantime. Besides, he didn't want to spoil what was a new source of income for the future. This last one had been worth a great deal of money. Frankly he could never understand how his clients were prepared to spend so much money on what was commonly known as art. It didn't do a thing for him, but each to his own. Now if it was horseflesh he could understand it. He had a couple of racehorses that showed promise. His one wish in life was to win the Derby. Now that would be something that would really give him pleasure.

Seven

The following day, Johnny rang his father. 'I thought we had agreed that you would hold back on the burglaries!' He accused the older man.

'I said I'd take your warnings on board! Listen, son, you're well covered, I saw to that but the timing was perfect and God knows when we'd have had the opportunity again. I couldn't let it go. Anyway, you have a watertight alibi, so what's your problem?'

'My problem is George Coleman! He threatened me in the club, said if he discovered any connection with the burglaries, I wouldn't make old bones!'

He heard his father laugh. 'Well he won't find any, so for heaven's sake relax. It'll be some time before we pull another stroke in Southampton, so stop getting your knees in a twist. Work on the girl, that's what you're good at!' And he hung up.

Johnny walked up and down his office, fuming, but he knew his father was the boss, what he said was never questioned and he was a past master when it came to criminal activities, which was why he'd never been caught. But it made Johnny nervous. He was enjoying being his own boss in Southampton, away from the tight hold Pat usually held over him. He was successful in the construction business and was quite enjoying being apart from the gangster life style he'd been brought up with. He was making money and he'd found a woman who really interested him, not just one who was an easy lay. He respected Victoria Teglia . . . but he lusted after her too. That made her even more interesting and he intended to keep after her for his own ends, not because his father told him to.

Whilst young Daniels was making his own plans, in Portsmouth, Bruce Chapman, in his office, was making his. He folded the papers on his desk and, putting them in a drawer, sat back and lit a cigarette. He had been ashore for a few weeks now and he missed the feel of a swaying ship beneath his feet. Were it not for the fact that he had renewed his relationship with Victoria, he would be really restless.

Getting up from his seat he wandered outside and breathed deeply, trying to fill his lungs with the smell of the salt air of the sea as he gazed over the Channel, looking at the naval ships sitting in the docks, some undergoing repairs, others preparing to sail. It was only the fact that he knew he would be given another vessel of his own in the near future that helped keep his sanity. That and Victoria, of course.

He smiled to himself as he thought of her. Her laughter, the scent of her warm body as he held her in his arms. The past they shared, the fun they had together. If only she would agree to marry him he would be a very happy man. He frowned. He could understand that she was enamoured with her new venture. After all, she'd worked hard to get the Club Valletta up and running and its success was mainly due to her personality and business acumen and he admired her for that, but he wanted more. How could he persuade her she could have both? If he was to be away, she'd need something to keep her occupied. Victoria had a restless spirit and being a stay-at-home wife would drive her crazy, until she had a family, of course, then it would be different, but was she ready for that yet? He didn't think so. Well, there was no rush, she was young; they could wait a while if that's what she wanted.

He walked back into his office and picked up the telephone, dialled a number and waited for a reply.

'Can I speak to Miss Teglia, please, it's Captain Chapman calling.' He waited.

'Hello, darling! Listen I'm going round the bend here, how about I drive over to Southampton this evening and we go out to dinner somewhere, then back to your place. I'm in need of comfort! Being in the navy is a lonely existence and I need nurturing.' He heard her chuckle on the end of the line.

Victoria was delighted to hear from Bruce. She knew he'd been busy and so had she and she welcomed the opportunity for a change.

'That would be lovely, Bruce. I thought you'd gone off with some young woman from your office.'

'As if I would dream of such a thing!'

They arranged to meet at the club, later that evening.

Bruce arrived on time and greeted Victoria warmly, kissing her soundly as they stood at the bar, to the delight of the female members of the staff, who eyed the good-looking captain with some envy.

'Bruce!' Victoria protested. 'Think of my position.'

He raised his eyebrows. 'Well, if you insist.'

'Come on, let's go before you embarrass me further.'

Outside, they climbed into his car and drove to the Cowherds Inn on the common, a large expanse of land with lakes, and wide open spaces where on bank holidays the fair would set up their stalls and rides to entertain the locals.

They were taken to a table in the far part of the dining room, affording them a modicum of privacy, and handed the menu. They ordered a starter and fish as their main course. Bruce chose a bottle of wine and then smiled at his companion.

'You look lovely,' he said softly.

'And you look very handsome; a man in uniform always has that something extra I always think.'

He laughed. 'It's the gold braid, darling, it gets the ladies every time!'

The chatted easily, catching up with each other's news, enjoying their dinner and relaxing when suddenly, over Bruce's shoulder, Victoria saw a figure approaching the table, grinning broadly at her.

'Good evening, Victoria,' said Johnny Daniels. 'What a pleasant surprise to find you here.' He nodded at Bruce then turned back to his companion. 'Looking as ravishing as ever. We must drive out to the New Forest again sometime soon. Enjoy your meal.' And he walked away.

Bruce gazed at Victoria, his jaw set. 'The New Forest? Well, it would seem you haven't been as busy as you led me to believe!'

'Oh, that was ages ago. Johnny is a member of the club and invited me to lunch as he'd been busy and needed a break and wondered if I needed one too, that's all.' But she could feel her cheeks flush as she spoke.

'Well, he's a cheeky bastard, coming on to you like that, right in front of me.' He looked at her quizzically. 'So, do you intend to accept his invitation?'

'Of course not! He called at a time when I needed a change of scene and I enjoyed getting out of the town for a day. That's all, Bruce!'

He let the matter drop, but it had unnerved him. He knew he was ready to settle down but perhaps Victoria was not and that was a concern. However he didn't want to spoil the first evening they'd spent together for some time and made no further mention of the encounter.

Later, when they were in bed together, he nibbled her ear and kissed her. 'Are you my girl, Victoria?'

'Of course I am, why ever did you ask?'

'I just like to know where I stand in your life. I know what I want but I'm damned if I know what's in your mind.'

She smiled provocatively. 'You must know what's in my mind, darling, I'm lying here naked, for goodness' sake!'

'That's not what I mean and you know it,' he said, insistently. 'Tonight at the Cowherds with that young man, I wondered if I was barking up the wrong tree, that's all. I'd much rather know now than find out later.'

She put her arms around his neck. 'Bruce, darling, do stop nattering like an old woman and make love to me . . . please.'

He knew it wasn't an answer, but how could he resist? It would have to do for now, but he wasn't going to give up Victoria without a fight, not to any man.

★　★　★

The following morning, when Victoria returned to the club, it was to find a large bouquet of flowers had been delivered to her. Curious, she took out the card and read it.

Hope I didn't get you into trouble last night? But you looked so lovely I couldn't resist saying hello. Johnny.

Shaking her head, she couldn't help but chuckle. This man was outrageous! But that was part of his attraction, of course. Although she knew that Johnny could cause trouble between her and Bruce if she encouraged him, she couldn't help but relish the situation. What woman wouldn't enjoy the attention of two men at the same time? It was flattering. Bruce, she felt deep down, *was* her future and Johnny Daniels was a dangerous game – if she was to play it. Knowing this made it the more inviting. Besides, she wasn't ready to settle down yet. She'd enjoyed the freedom the navy had given her, away from parental control. She'd enjoyed the odd affair before Bruce came into her life. During her navy days she felt she'd grown up, become a woman in her own right and now with her own business, she was wholly independent and didn't have to answer to anyone. But if she became engaged to Bruce her freedom would be curtailed and she wasn't ready to relinquish it just yet.

Despite their extensive enquiries, the Southampton police had been unable to shed light on the burglary at Chilworth and Henry Charterhouse was not happy when he called into the police station to talk to the detective in charge of the case.

Detective Inspector Black tried to explain. 'I'm really sorry, sir, but the perpetrators were professionals. No fingerprints, the alarm had been doctored when they called supposedly to service it, and so it didn't go off here when they entered the building.'

'But there were no signs of a break in.' Henry said, inter-rupting, 'which would have alerted my housekeeper when she returned.'

'One can only assume they had the tools to pick the lock on the front door and they knew what they came for. After all, they left a lot of valuable stuff behind.' He scratched his chin. 'I would say they had a buyer all lined up for the books and the painting. A private collector, of course, one that won't be showing off his latest acquisition to anyone, that's for sure. I trust you were insured?'

'Of course I was, I'm not an idiot! Now the premiums will go sky high.'

'We'll keep our enquiries open, but frankly, Mr Charterhouse, I don't think there's much hope of you getting the stuff back. I'm sorry, sir.'

Henry left the police station and made his way to his friend's house in Basset. Roger Bentley was one of his friends who regularly played roulette at the Club Valletta. He was a wealthy barrister and his house was furnished with priceless antiques. He had an office in London but worked from home when he could. He welcomed his friend into the house.

'Be with you in a moment, old chap, I'm just talking to Mr Daniels about some work I need done on the roof. You may have seen him at the club, come along in, I'm nearly done.'

Henry followed him into the impressive drawing room.

'Just been to the police station.' Henry complained. 'They haven't a damned clue about what happened to the things that were stolen from my place.'

Johnny Daniels caught his breath as he overheard the conversation as the men entered the room.

'Daniels, do you know Henry Charterhouse?'

Johnny smiled a greeting. 'No, we haven't been introduced, but of course I've seen you both there together, chancing your luck in the gaming room.'

'Well, poor Henry's luck ran out when he was burgled. I expect you read about it in the *Echo?*'

'Yes, yes I did. Terrible business.'

'Well I hope your security is tight here, Roger,' his friend remarked.

'But didn't I read that your housekeeper let two men in who said they'd come to see to the alarm?' Johnny casually asked.

Henry mumbled angrily. 'They showed her their credentials which looked all right. Can't blame her for that. Clever sods!'

Johnny just wanted to leave before he became too involved in talking about this further, knowing that it was his father's men who'd pulled the job.

'Right, Mr Bentley, I'll get my men here on Wednesday of next week. We'll soon get the roof back in shape. It shouldn't take too long.' And he made his escape.

Outside, sitting in his car, he breathed a sigh of relief. That was too close for comfort and he cursed his father. He wouldn't feed him any more information, he decided. It would only screw up his reputation if his clients got wind of his background and he had a lot of business lined up in the forthcoming weeks.

Once back in his office, he rang the club and asked to speak to Victoria. He felt the need for a bit of fun after his encounter and there was only one companion he wanted to share this with.

'Hello?' Victoria answered the phone herself.

'Miss Teglia, this is your secret admirer speaking,' he said, teasing her.

'Johnny! Thank you for the beautiful flowers.'

'You're very welcome . . . did I get you into trouble with the handsome captain?'

'You did that on purpose, coming over to the table and talking about the New Forest. You are truly wicked!'

He could hear the amusement in her voice. 'Well, he looked far too comfortable; I thought a shock would do him good.'

'Oh, Johnny, what am I going to do with you?'

'Come out with me, let's go and have some fun together. I'm feeling restless.'

'What had you in mind?'

'Miss Teglia, you really don't want to know what's in my mind, but I'll settle for your company and a meal. Let's drive out to Hamble, we can look at the boats and have lunch, overlooking the water. What do you say?'

'When?'

'Are you free now?'

Victoria hesitated before answering, knowing she should refuse, but it was the beginning of the week when lunchtime trade was slow. She could easily get away and she made up her mind. Why not? It was only lunch.

'All right, give me half an hour and I'll be free.'

'I'll wait outside for you,' he replied. He didn't want Coleman glaring at him if he waited for her inside the club. The man made him uncomfortable.

They drove out to Hamble, chatting about inconsequential things until Johnny parked the car and they walked around the jetties looking at the various boats moored there.

'Have you ever wanted one of these yachts?' Victoria asked.

'No, not me! The sea is a dangerous element; you have to know what you're doing on a boat. Besides, in a heavy sea, I don't like the way the yachts lean over and look as if they're going to capsize. Four wheels and a motor will do thank you.'

They sauntered back to the inn and ordered lunch. It was reasonably quiet and they had a table overlooking the water.

'Must be nice living round here,' he said, somewhat wistfully.

'I thought you were a city boy, coming as you do from London.'

'I like London, don't misunderstand me. It has a buzz about it and the theatres . . . but it's noisy and dirty. Here, it's clean and peaceful. A pleasant change.'

She looked at him quizzically. 'You never fail to surprise me.'

'In what way?'

'You mentioned the theatres. I wouldn't have thought you'd be interested in such things.'

'You know nothing about me, Victoria, but it's obvious that you've already made up your mind as to the sort of person I am and that's hardly fair!'

'So who are you? Tell me.'

'That's no fun at all.' He was teasing her again. 'If we were to see more of each other, think how many surprises you might have.'

'There might be some I wouldn't like,' she said, looking at him with twinkling eyes.

'You'll never know until you try,' he said, laughing at her. Then, handing her the menu, he asked, 'Would you like a dessert?'

After their meal he drove her along a narrow lane and parked the car in a deserted area, overlooking the Solent where the passing ships showed on the horizon and several yachts were sailing by. He put an arm around her shoulders and slowly and deliberately pulled her towards him.

'You, Victoria Teglia, are a very desirable woman!' And he kissed her.

Victoria closed her eyes as his mouth explored hers. His hands caressing her, sending shivers down her spine. She knew she shouldn't be enjoying this, but she was and she returned his kisses with a fervency that surprised her.

When eventually he released her, he gazed into her eyes. 'That was even better than I envisaged,' he said softly, and kissed her again.

As his caresses became more ardent, Victoria broke away from his hold.

'We need to go,' she gasped, breathlessly

'You don't really mean that,' he coaxed.

'Yes, Johnny, I do.'

He didn't argue further, but turned on the ignition, put the car into gear and drove back to the club. Neither of them exchanged a word during the journey, both lost in their own thoughts. Johnny was pleased with his progress with this lovely woman whilst Victoria was surprised at her own passion in the arms of this fascinating man, whom she felt could completely unsettle her life.

Johnny pulled up and parked outside the Club Valletta and, turning towards Victoria, kissed her briefly. 'I'll see you soon,' he said.

'I'm not sure that's such a good idea,' she replied.

He caressed her cheek. 'You know you don't really mean that.'

She didn't reply and got out of the car and walked away.

He watched until she'd entered the club, then he drove back to his office with a smile of satisfaction. There would be another time, of that he was certain.

Eight

'What do you mean he hasn't come up with the rest of the money?' Pat Daniels demanded as he sat at the desk of his London dockland office.

One of his men stood before him and tried to explain, somewhat nervously. Daniels was not a man to upset even if you were a member of his gang of criminals.

'As you know, he paid half the money for the books up front and was coming to London with the rest of the cash, but he sent a message to say he was too busy and couldn't get away.'

'Too fucking busy! Who does he think he's dealing with?' Pat swiped the papers off his desk in anger then he picked up the telephone and dialled. 'You know who this is and I'll give you seven days to come up with the dosh you owe me. If you fail you'll have to face the consequences.' He slammed the receiver down.

On the wall was a calendar. He rose from his chair and marked a cross against the date, seven days hence. 'He'd better come across or he'll be very sorry,' he told his man. 'He thinks because he lives in Scotland it's too far away from me to have to worry. Well he couldn't be more wrong! Now he'll have to pay interest on the days he's late and he won't like that. Well tough! I'll be up his arse before he knows it.'

As the man left the room, Pat sat and fumed. These people with money thought they could treat him like some minion. He wasn't some small-time hoodlum, he was a man with a lot of power as some who'd tried to cross him in the past had found, to their detriment. A Scottish laird was just another customer, his wealth and title didn't mean a thing. It didn't make him foolproof. Accepting stolen goods, to satisfy his own ego, made him just as much a criminal as any other who broke the law, so all the airs and graces in the world wouldn't make any difference to the outcome. If he tried to welch on a deal, it would not be tolerated.

Victoria's mother, Lily, was also busy on the phone, talking to George Coleman, keeping check on Johnny.

'What's the situation between my daughter and Johnny Daniels?' she asked her old friend.

'He sent her flowers the other day because I made it my business to look at the card and, although Victoria didn't tell me, she went out with him yesterday. I saw him waiting outside. She was only gone for a few hours. Maybe he took her out to lunch,' he told her. 'Naturally I didn't question her on her return. I didn't want her to think I was spying.'

'No of course not,' said Lily. 'I think it's time she knows about his background. I'll be in touch.'

She sat quietly pondering the situation. Victoria should know who she was dealing with, she decided, before she became too involved with the young man. Charm or no charm, his background was one she didn't want Victoria anywhere near. She must warn her now, before it was too late and, to this end, that evening she rang the club and invited Victoria to go shopping with her the next day.

Victoria was looking forward to a day spent with her mother, whom she adored. With both of them being in business, they didn't see so much of each other these days and they always had such fun together.

The two women trawled the shops looking for dresses that didn't scream utility. They bought odd items of make-up and ended up in a hat shop, trying on all the models, before purchasing one each, in the knowledge that millinery didn't require clothing coupons.

'Come on,' said Lily, 'I'm famished. Let's get something to eat. We'll go to Gatti's. I know the head waiter there; he'll rustle up something special.'

Victoria laughed. 'There aren't many people in the town that you don't know, Mother.'

'And very useful it is too, you'll see.'

They were escorted to a table by the head waiter who greeted

Lily warmly and who suggested she leave the choice of menu to him, which she readily agreed to. Consequently, they ate very well.

As they tucked into a very fine steak, Victoria said, 'This is delicious, I wonder where the chef found this supply?'

'Best not to ask,' Lily chided. 'I expect your chef has a few secrets up his sleeve, I know mine has. I never question him, it's better that way.'

After dessert, they ordered coffee and a liqueur and Lily asked after Bruce.

'Have you seen the handsome captain lately?'

'Yes, we had lunch together a few days ago. He's fine, busy and if the truth be known, he can't wait to be given his own ship again. Bruce is truly a man of the sea.'

'That means he'll be away, won't you miss him? After all, you both seem to be very close.'

'Of course I'll miss him, but, as you know, the club keeps me occupied, so it won't be quite so bad.'

'And of course you'll have that dashing Johnny Daniels hanging around, to keep you from getting bored!' She stared at her daughter, trying to read her reaction.

Victoria blushed, which filled Lily with some trepidation.

'Johnny is a member, that's all.'

'You have never been able to lie to me, Victoria, so don't start now. I can understand you being attracted to him, for goodness' sake. I've been in your shoes when I was younger and the dangerous men were always the most interesting.'

'He's not dangerous!' Victoria protested.

'No? His father is known as Big Pat Daniels. He's a known criminal and works out of London Docks. He's in the same construction business as his son, all quite legitimate. It's a good front for his criminal activities.' She saw the shocked look on Victoria's face. 'How do you know that Johnny Daniels isn't setting up the same down here? A new family branch, if you like.'

Victoria didn't know what to say. All this had come as a terrible shock to her. Deep down she'd always had a feeling that there was a dangerous streak in Johnny but she had never envisaged a criminal one. She'd just thought it was because he was attractive and would be like a magnet to women. But a criminal?

'How do you know all this?' she demanded.

'I made it my business to know after George found out about his father. He never trusted Johnny from the beginning.'

Now Victoria was furious. 'You've both been spying on me!'

'No, we have been looking after you! Do you want to become part of this young man's world and finish up like your father?'

'You became part of it!' Her eyes flashed angrily.

'Yes, I did. At the time I had no choice. But believe me, I knew it was a dangerous thing to do. Despite being attracted to your father, I would never have become involved with him if I had any other means of keeping life and soul together. I won't stand by and see you make the same mistake. You have a business, you can keep yourself and you have Luke and me . . . and you have Bruce, he would take care of you for the rest of your life, given the opportunity, I'm sure. You are in a different situation. You don't *need* Johnny Daniels!'

'I know you mean well, Mum, but I'm a big girl now. I can make my own decisions. I cut your apron strings when I joined the navy!'

Lily was deeply hurt by this remark, but she was determined to get her point across.

'Of course you are a grown woman and I'm immensely proud of what you've achieved, I just don't want to see it all go down the pan because of an unsuitable man.'

'I don't think of him like that and anyway, he can't help who his father is! It doesn't mean to say he's the same.'

'This is true, but you need to know about his background, that's all. After all, darling, forewarned is forearmed.' And she dropped the subject. The joyful atmosphere had changed though and the two of them parted company soon after.

Lily walked back to her hotel without real regret, only that Victoria was angry with her, but that she could live with. She felt she had done her duty as a mother, now the decision was her daughter's. She couldn't run her life for her after all – but she could watch her back.

Victoria walked slowly, trying to make sense of the information she'd been given. She wanted to believe that Johnny was not like his father, but now she couldn't help but wonder if the burglary at Henry Charterhouse's had anything to do with him? Was he in the same business as his father and setting up his own branch of the business here in Southampton as her mother had suggested? Her thoughts were in turmoil. Yes, she was attracted to him and when he'd held her and kissed her, she'd enjoyed it far too much.

In his small flat in London, Sandy was feeling restless. He was tired of the city, his latest amour had dumped him and he felt in need of a change. He packed a bag and caught a train to Southampton. It would be nice to visit a few old friends, see Lily and Victoria and visit some old haunts. There he could relax. It would be like old times, but better. He'd saved a bit of money for his retirement. After all, he didn't want to play piano in pubs for very much longer. He wanted to enjoy the years left to him. Perhaps he could find a cheap flat and move back to the town which held so many memories.

It was with great surprise that Victoria saw her old friend walk through the doors of the club just as the lunchtime trade was nearing its end. She rushed forward to greet Sandy.

'What are you doing here, you old reprobate?' she asked, giving him a hug.

'I decided I needed a holiday so I'm down for a week. Got a room free I can stay in?'

'As a matter of fact I have. A nice single which will suit you very well, but first let me buy you a drink.'

'I thought you'd never ask.' He walked with her to the bar. As he did so, George Coleman saw him and wandered over. The men shook hands.

'Haven't seen you for ages, Sandy, how's things?'

'Not bad, but I'm weary of the old life. I'm thinking of retiring.'

'You are? Victoria chipped in. 'I thought you'd be pressing the keys until you kicked the bucket.'

Sandy sipped the beer he'd ordered. 'No, darling, I want a bit of fun in my life before then and as they say, only the good die young, I reckon I've got a few years left!'

Laughing, she asked, 'How long do you want to stay?'

'About a week I should think, is that all right?'

She put an arm round his shoulders. 'Of course, no problem. You'll be my guest. It'll be lovely having you around. Look, it's quiet now so why don't you join me for lunch?'

'Thanks, I am hungry. I didn't stop for breakfast other than a cup of coffee.'

Whilst they ate, Sandy asked about the business, her mother and all the gossip that was available and he told her about his life in London. 'I may look around for a flat to rent while I'm here,' he told her. 'I'm getting tired of working for a living, I want to take some time to sniff the daisies and what better place than Southampton?' They ate and enjoyed an hour or so of hilarious conversation.

After lunch Victoria took him to his room. 'Let me know if you need anything. I'm off home until this evening but you only have to ask the staff, they'll look after you until I come back later.'

Sandy unpacked, then he took a walk around the streets of Southampton's docklands, somewhat changed after the Blitz, but to him still full of nostalgia and he knew that he would come back and stay permanently. This was where he belonged.

Later that evening he walked downstairs and sat at the bar, reading the *Southern Evening Echo,* catching up with local news and the programmes being shown at the cinemas in the town.

Victoria arrived and they were sitting and talking when the club door opened and Johnny Daniels entered. He walked over to them and slapped Sandy on the back.

'You are a bit out of your way aren't you?'

Victoria looked from one to the other. 'How do you two know each other?'

'Johnny and his father use the pub I play in,' Sandy told her.

This bit of information intrigued Victoria after the conversation she'd had with her mother and she was delighted. What better person than Sandy to be able to answer the questions that plagued her mind about this young man? She decided to put them to him after the club closed. At least she would get an honest answer about Johnny's character and if anyone knew if he was involved in the underworld it would be Sandy.

'Well, Miss Teglia,' said Johnny, 'you're looking marvellous as ever. When am I to have the pleasure of your company again?'

Looking at him she couldn't help remembering how she had felt being held in his arms. She felt her cheeks flush. 'At the moment I'm really busy,' she told him.

He smiled softly. 'I can wait . . . as long as I have to.'

Sandy looked intrigued. What had been going on between these two?

Victoria quickly excused herself and Johnny sat on the stool beside Sandy, who looked at the young man mischievously.

'That wouldn't be the good girl you spoke about by any chance?'

The young man chuckled. 'Nothing gets past you does it you old devil? As a matter of fact it is. I think she's marvellous and I do believe she likes me a little.'

'She's far too good to be just another conquest.' Sandy ventured quietly.

'Believe me, Sandy, this one is special. She's definitely in a class of her own. How do you know her?'

'I'm a good friend of her mother and I've known Victoria from the day she was born. I've watched her grow up and she's very dear to me and you need to know that!'

Johnny raised his eyebrows quizzically. 'You warning me off by any chance?'

'I'm telling you to treat her right, that's all.'

'Her mother told me the same thing not so very long ago. Now there's a formidable woman.'

'You take my advice, young man, tread carefully or the wrath of God will descend on you and you'll wonder what hit you!'

'George Coleman, you mean? He really doesn't like me, he made that very clear some time ago.'

'Then, young Johnny, you are treading on very dangerous ground. Be warned. Now I'm off to search out a few of my favourite drinking places. I'll see you again soon.'

Daniels sat pondering the conversation he'd had with the pianist, but, nevertheless, nothing was going to stop him seeing Victoria Teglia, not even her father's right-hand man. He looked at his watch, drank up and, seeing Victoria across the room, he caught her gaze, blew a kiss in her direction and left the club.

Victoria looked for Sandy but he wasn't there. She couldn't wait to put a million questions to him before she went to bed that night. She wanted answers. Good or bad, she needed to know the truth.

Nine

Sandy returned to the club just before it closed, a little the worse for wear. He'd trawled the pubs he used to frequent that were still standing and had met several old friends. It had been a good night.

Victoria saw the somewhat glazed look in the eyes of her friend and sent a waiter for a pot of black coffee. 'Here,' she said when it was served, 'get some of this down you or you'll have a hell of a hangover tomorrow morning.'

His words were slightly slurred as he grinned at her. 'Thank you, Mother! I've had such a good time tonight. Thank God most of my old pals are still about. Mind you –' he leaned closer – 'they haven't worn as well as me, darling!'

Victoria sent for a tray of sandwiches also. She needed to sober him up before she could pump him about the Danielses. But slightly inebriated he might be more forthcoming with his information.

Eventually she posed her first question. 'Tell me about Johnny Daniels and especially his father. He's never mentioned him in any of our conversations.'

Sandy had sobered up enough to know what was going on and he thought for a moment about how much he should tell her – and decided on the truth.

'Don't suppose he has, he wouldn't want you to know about Big Pat.'

'Why not?'

'Because he's a villain, that's why. In London, the underworld treats him with respect and leaves him and his patch alone.'

'What do you mean, his patch?' Victoria was now intrigued.

'All villains have their own territory, darling, and believe me they don't invite tourists from another gang. That's a dangerous game to play.'

'Does Johnny belong to this world too? Is he a villain? Tell me the truth, Sandy, I need to know.'

'To be honest, Victoria, I'm not sure. He worked with his father in the construction business until he knew enough to start up on his own. How much involved he was in the other side of the trade I don't know. And that's the truth. However, a few weeks ago he was up in London talking to his dad and I just felt that something was going down. A gut reaction, that's all.'

She frowned as she asked, 'Can you remember when this happened?

When Sandy told her, she realized it was just before Henry Charterhouse was burgled and she paled. 'Oh my God,' she muttered.

'What is it, Victoria?' asked Sandy.

She told him of her fears and asked, 'Do you think Johnny set it up?'

'Was he questioned by the police, do you know?'

She shrugged. 'No, but then he wouldn't tell me, would he?'

'If he knew about it, no doubt he had a watertight alibi. These men are so bloody clever, that's why Daniels senior is still walking the streets; no one has been able to pin anything on him. He's a clever bugger!'

'Is Johnny anything like his father?'

'No, darling, I'm happy to say he isn't. Pat is a hard case; he hasn't an ounce of charm in the whole of his body, unlike young Lochinvar!' He paused. 'You like him, don't you, Victoria?'

'Yes, Sandy, I do.' She hesitated. 'There's something about him that I find intriguing. I can't help it — and what's more I know it's unwise.'

He caught hold of her hand. 'Sadly the most enjoyable things in life are unwise, darling. Look, I'm bushed; I need to get my head down. Just be careful, that's all.' He kissed her cheek and made his way to his room.

Victoria poured herself some coffee and mulled over her conversation. Her mother had been right all along, but now what? Not only did she have her own feelings to consider but she had the responsibility to her clients to safeguard them and their belongings. If Johnny was using her club to line up victims for his father, she'd have to put a stop to it. There was only one thing to do and that was confront him.

The following morning, she rang Johnny's office and said she wanted to meet him that day.

He was delighted. 'Well, Victoria, this is a surprise, but a very pleasant one. Where would you like to go? Just say the word.'

She thought quickly. It needed to be somewhere quiet and private. 'You know the lake beside the Cowherds Inn?'

Somewhat puzzled he said he did.

'Then I'll meet you there in twenty minutes.' She ordered a taxi and left her flat.

Meanwhile, Johnny got into his car and drove along the avenue to the common. He parked the car outside the Cowherds and walked to the lake, where he saw Victoria feeding the swans.

'Hello, gorgeous,' he said as he kissed her cheek. 'Why here?'

'Because it's quiet and we can talk undisturbed.'

'There was something in the tone of her voice that made him realize that this was not the romantic meeting he'd thought it was going to be. They walked to a bench and sat down.

'What's on your mind, Victoria, because something certainly is?'

She was very direct. 'Did you have anything to do with the burglary at Henry Charterhouse's home?' She stared into his eyes waiting for a response.

'What?' This was not what he expected and he knew he had to think quickly to allay her suspicions. 'What on earth are you talking about?'

Victoria was not a fool and she saw him stiffen slightly when she asked the question. 'I know all about your father, Johnny, so please don't pretend you're innocent.'

He knew immediately that Sandy had been talking to her.

'My father is his own man, what he does has nothing to do with me! I run a legitimate business and I'm really hurt that you should think I had anything at all to do with that incident.'

She was unfazed by his denial. 'Let's face it, Johnny, you have the perfect cover. Yes, I know you do good work. After all, several of my clients at the club speak highly of you, but how convenient for you. How easy it is for you to choose the members who are wealthy who have houses stuffed with valuable objects. Things that would bring in a lot of money if they were given to a fence to sell.'

He started to laugh. 'Oh, Victoria, you've been reading too many thrillers. Yes, it would be a great set up, but a very dangerous one if it were true. How long do you think I could get away with such a thing? Not very long before two and two would make four.'

He put an arm round her shoulders, but he could feel the rigidity in her body. 'Tell me you don't really believe me capable of such a thing.' He held her gaze, willing her to believe him.

She stared back at him but his gaze didn't falter and for a moment she was confused. Could she be wrong? Was it possible that he was telling the truth? She wanted to believe him, but dare she?'

'If I thought for one moment you had anything at all to do with this, I'd report you to the authorities! I've worked my fingers to the bone to make the club a success and if you did anything to destroy it, I would really make you pay.'

For one moment, Johnny could see why her father, Vittorio Teglia, was a feared man. This was no idle threat, his daughter meant every word and he knew if she was proved right, she'd set out to destroy him – without hesitation.

'Victoria, darling, I would never do anything to hurt you, honestly. Don't you realize that I'm falling in love with you?'

She felt her resolve weaken – but only for a moment. 'Don't think you can sweet talk me, Johnny, because it won't work. Just be warned, that's all.'

'You have my word, I had nothing to do with it,' he lied. 'If I recall correctly, on that day I was in the docks, waiting for a shipment. The customs and docks police can vouch for that, should you care to ask.'

'How very convenient!' Her tone was like ice. 'But you still see your father. If you have nothing to do with his crimes, why do you visit him?'

'My father has never been imprisoned or charged for any crime, Victoria, so you're taking a lot for granted!'

'Neither was mine but he was still a villain and I know because I've learned from others when I was older that he broke the law many times but was too clever to be caught.'

'Then you should understand my position. I'm not answerable for my father, Victoria. I run my own life and I'm very proud of what I've achieved, as you are with your work. You are not your father's daughter after all, only by blood, as am I with mine!'

She so wanted to believe him, but she was still uncertain.

Seeing this uncertainty in her expression, Johnny leaned forward and kissed her softly. 'Feeling the way I do about you, Victoria, why would I do anything to hurt you?'

She had no answer.

'Come on, I need a drink. I feel as if I've been through the third degree and I'm sure you could do with one too.' He stood up and held out his hand.

Victoria hesitated but eventually she took it and they walked together to the Cowherds Inn where they sat quietly in a corner.

'I meant what I said about the way I feel about you, you know. That wasn't a load of bull.' He looked earnestly at her realizing that indeed he spoke the truth. He'd never felt like this about any of the many women who'd wandered through his life. It wasn't only lust with him, now it was much deeper and that made things very difficult. He had to stop his father from pulling any more jobs in Southampton. But how was he going to do it? It would be like trying to move a mountain.

Victoria was nonplussed by his declaration. She was still uncertain about this young man who was a complete enigma, but she knew he'd got into her blood and it would be difficult to keep away from him.

'Don't you feel anything for me, Victoria? Have I been getting the wrong signals?'

'To be honest I don't know. Let's leave it at that for now.'

'All right if that's the way you want it.'

They drank up and left the Inn. He walked her to his car, drew her into his arms and kissed her with a longing that he felt in his loins. He couldn't lose this girl. He wanted her in his life, but first he'd have to sort out his father.

He drove her back to the club, then returned to his office.

The next day, Johnny took a train to London and caught a taxi to his father's home, where he'd asked to meet him.

Pat Daniels was curious. His son usually met him at his local so what was going on in the boy's head? He hoped he wasn't going to try and cause a problem with his organization. No, the lad knew better than to try to interfere. Perhaps he needed money for his business.

He looked up as Johnny walked into the living room. 'Hello, son, what's on your mind?'

Johnny sat down and faced his father. 'I'm sorry, Dad, but you have to cancel any plans you have to turn over the other two addresses I gave you in Southampton.'

Pat looked coldly at his son. 'Really! And why's that?'

'Because I want out. I want to be legitimate from now on.'

This was the last thing the older man was expecting and he started to laugh derisively.

'Bloody hell! What's got into you? Have you found God or something?'

'No, but I've found a girl and I'm doing well in business, I'm able to make a good living and I don't need to be part of your world any more. I want to be able to live my life without having to watch my back all the time, wondering when I'm going to feel the strong arm of the law on my shoulder.'

'You going soft or what?' Pat was furious.

'No, Dad, but I want to settle down in the future, have a family, and not have them worry, as Mum has done all these years.'

'Your mother has never complained and neither have you, my boy! Since you were old enough, you were happy to come along with me and reap the benefits, as I recall.' He looked his son up and down. 'How could you afford to dress so well in these austere days if you didn't have the money to pay a good tailor for the clothing coupons you didn't have. The cars you ran with the extra petrol I found – at a price. The money you earned from the profits to tempt the women you liked so much!'

But Johnny was determined. 'You're right and I admit all that, but now I want a different kind of life. If you turn those two places over, my position in Southampton will be jeopardized and I could lose my girl. What's more, if she thinks I have anything to do with it, she'll shop me to the police.'

Pat looked perturbed. 'What do you mean?'

Johnny told him about his conversation with Victoria.

'Ah, the Teglia girl, I should have known. Strange, don't you think, her father was as big a villain as me and as hard, I'd have thought she'd be up for our sort of business.'

'Don't be bloody ridiculous! Her father died when she was a baby, she's never been part of our world!'

Pat's face flushed with anger. 'Don't you use that tone with me, boy! You show a bit more respect!' He sat back in his chair wondering just how to handle this unexpected situation. His son was as stubborn as he was and he knew that if Johnny wanted out, there was no way he could persuade him otherwise, but he had no intention of losing two such prize jobs.

'Very well. I'll give you six months leeway. If at the end of that time, you feel the same, we'll shake hands and part company. Until then, you keep away from me. After all, I can't have you hanging around listening to my plans, can I?'

Johnny looked across the table at his father. 'Isn't it time you retired, Dad, and just ran the construction business? I don't want to see you end up behind bars.'

Pat looked coldly at him. 'Don't preach to me, son. You want to live your life your way, then I suggest you leave me to live mine!' He rose from his seat. 'We're done here.' He left the house, slamming the door behind him.

Johnny let out a sigh of relief. This had been the hardest thing he'd ever done and it had gone better than he'd hoped. No one ever crossed his father, he'd seen what had happened to those who'd tried and he'd had no way of knowing how Pat would react. Never the less, he knew his father well and knew if he'd lined up the jobs in Southampton, nothing he could say would change his mind, but he'd had to try. Now he'd have to ensure that the two victims he'd lined up for his father were safeguarded, which was going to be very tricky for him to organize without causing suspicion.

Ten

Two days later, Daniels made his way to Roger Bentley's house to check on the men working on the roof at a time when he knew his client would be home. They walked round the opulent building together, discussing the work, after which Roger invited Johnny inside for a coffee to discuss another job he wanted doing.

They sat in the large drawing room and Johnny admired the beautiful antique furniture. 'After the bad experience your friend Mr Charterhouse had, aren't you worried about being burgled too?'

Bentley smiled. 'I have a very good alarm system and it's wired straight through to the local police station. And my staff have orders not to let anyone into the house on any pretence unless I'm here. It's worked very well up until now.'

'How long has this system been installed, if you don't mind me asking?'

'Two years.'

Johnny's heart sank knowing that his father and his gang would have full knowledge of such a system. 'May I make a suggestion, Mr Bentley?'

'Of course.'

Johnny had a friend who was a genius at electronics and before he left London he'd called on him only to be shown his latest invention . . . a new alarm system. 'I deny anyone to beat it, Johnny,' his friend had told him. 'It's been patented and the first ones have just been produced.' Johnny had bought two.

He told Roger Bentley about it and suggested he had it installed as well as the old one. 'Then you have absolute protection against intruders! Give it a try, you have nothing to lose by it and it will give you that extra edge. It's so new that anyone trying to break in will not be familiar with it, whereas they might know the workings of the other. What do you say?'

'As long as I keep the old one, I'm prepared to give it a try, why not?'

'You might mention it to your friend who lives in Romsey, too. It's too late for poor Mr Charterhouse but not for him, and if you are pleased it will help my friend sell his invention.'

'You on some sort of commission, Daniels?' The barrister laughed.

'No, sir, just helping out an old friend, that's all. He has such an amazing brain but you know these clever devils, they are not business minded and I offered to help him get established, that's all.'

The alarm was installed that day.

Whilst Johnny was trying to protect his position, Victoria was in London with Bruce. He'd called and asked her to spend the weekend with him in the metropolis, to get away from his work and hers. She, in a state of flux about her feelings for the young man who'd so upset her equilibrium, knew she needed to sort out her own feelings. After all, she had planned a future with Bruce in her own mind and now she needed to make a decision. She and Bruce had been lovers for a long time and she felt it wouldn't be fair to him to be so undecided. This weekend with him would get things into perspective, she hoped.

Bruce had booked them into the Ritz Hotel and had tickets for them to see a show. Apart from which they would be able to spend time together to recapture their relationship which he felt was wavering – and he didn't know why.

They were shown to their room on the first floor and Bruce suggested they find a restaurant and have lunch. 'Then we can decide what you'd like to do, darling,' he said.

Victoria looked around the beautifully furnished room and breathed a deep sigh.

Bruce took her into his arms. 'Good heavens, that came from your boots! What's wrong, tiger?'

She looked up at the face she knew so well and felt a pang of guilt. 'I was just thinking how wonderful it was being away from Southampton and work. Come on, let's eat, I'm famished.'

They found a small, sophisticated restaurant where they enjoyed fresh salmon served with a selection of vegetables, followed by a delicious gateau. After drinking a decent bottle of Chablis, followed by coffee, Victoria found she had totally relaxed. Bruce as always was a perfect companion. He regaled her with tales of his time in the navy that made her laugh. They reminisced about shared past experiences and she wondered how on earth she could ever have doubted her feelings for this man.

After, they wandered around the streets of London, window shopping, stopped later for tea and eventually wandered back to the hotel, to change for the evening show, after which Bruce planned for them to finish the night in a club he knew.

Once inside the room, Bruce took Victoria into his arms and kissed her.

'How long will it take you to get changed?' he asked.

'About half an hour,' she murmured, her face buried into his chest.

'Then we have plenty of time,' he said quietly and undid the zip at the back of her dress, slipping it off her shoulders. He nuzzled her neck, removed her bra and kissed her breasts, his hands caressing her back, sending shivers of anticipation down her spine. Lifting her he carried her to the bed, laid her down gently and removed his clothes.

She looked at his taught frame which she knew so well, knowing what pleasure was to be hers as he lay beside her and took her into his arms.

Their love making was slow and unhurried, giving each other time to respond to every caress, every intimate touch, every kiss, until neither could hold back any longer . . .

After, they lay in each other's arms, breathless and happy.

Bruce glanced at his watch. 'Much as I hate to break this up,' he murmured, 'we had better get dressed or we'll miss the show.'

Victoria raised herself reluctantly and kissed him. 'I won't be long,' she said and went to the bathroom.

Bruce sat on the end of the bed and lit a cigarette. Away from the club, Victoria seemed like the girl he once knew. Was he wrong to think something had changed between them? When he'd spoken to her lately on the telephone he'd felt she was distracted. Had that young man who'd come up to them when they were dining at the Cowherds Inn anything to do with it? There had definitely been a frisson of something between them, he'd thought. But just now, in his arms, Victoria had been as sensual with him as she'd always been. Nothing had changed there.

The West End debut of *An Inspector Calls* was a great success. Bruce and Victoria emerged from the theatre delighted with the play and caught a taxi to The Coconut Grove nightclub where Edmundo Ros and his orchestra were playing.

After dancing the rumba, they returned to their table. 'Oh, Bruce, that was such fun!' said Victoria as she sat down. 'I love Edmundo Ros's music. I have some of his records at home, not that I've had any time to play them lately.'

'Neither of us have had time to do anything but work, darling. It was time to relax, I'm glad you're happy.' He reached across the table and held her hand. 'You *are* happy aren't you, Victoria?'

She saw the uncertainty in his eyes and was angry with herself because she knew she was the cause. 'Of course I am, how could you think differently?'

Bruce decided not to push his luck as things seemed to be going so well. He topped up her glass from the bottle on the table. Picking up his glass he said, 'To us.'

She picked up hers. 'To us, Bruce darling!'

On Sunday, the following day, they took a boat up the Thames, walked along the Embankment and visited St Paul's Cathedral, climbing the stairs to the whispering gallery. Like an excited boy, Bruce walked to the other side and, leaning against the wall, asked, 'Can you hear me?'

Chuckling, Victoria said she could. She watched him go down on one knee and wondered what on earth he was doing. 'Victoria, darling, will you marry me?'

She didn't know what to say and hesitated.

'Say something, darling, I'm getting cramp here and I'm getting strange looks from a woman nearby who thinks I've lost my marbles . . . it isn't good for my credibility as a man!'

She burst out laughing. 'Yes, you fool, I will!' She watched him get to his feet, nod and smile to the woman who moved quickly away. Bruce gazed across the gallery and shrugged as if to say, I told you so.

As she waited for her lover to make his way back, Victoria thought, well, that's it. Problem solved. She did love Bruce, they were good together. He was someone she could rely on, would never let her down – and he made her laugh, which in this life was essential to survival, she always thought. She knew Lily, her mother would be delighted . . . and it did put everything into perspective which had been her reason for this break. Johnny Daniels would have no further place in her life other than as a member at the club. He was just a moment of madness, which every girl was entitled to. After all, they hadn't done anything more than exchanged a passionate kiss or two.

Bruce had returned and he took her into his arms, to the amusement of those few people standing near. 'Congratulations, darling, we've just got engaged! I'll buy you a ring when we get back to Southampton!'

There was a small round of applause from a small group who had overheard him.

He beamed at them. 'Thank you very much. She is such a lucky girl don't you think?' They all laughed, including Victoria.

That evening they went out to celebrate. Bruce ordered champagne and when it was poured, he held up his glass. 'You have made me a very happy man, tiger. To our future.'

'To our future,' she responded.

'I'll have to find out what plans the navy has for me before we can make a date for the wedding,' he told her.

'That's fine, Bruce, after all, there's no rush.'

He raised a quizzical eyebrow. 'I don't want us to hang around, darling. I want us to settle a date as soon as possible. We've wasted too much time as it is. You disappeared from my life once before, I don't want you to do that again!'

Smiling, she said, 'Why would I? Where would I go? I have a business to run.'

'Oh, thanks very much! I was expecting a more personal reason for you staying.'

Although his reproach was said with humour, she saw the hurt in his eyes.

'I didn't mean it quite as it sounded, I'm sorry.'

'It's all right. Besides, it will be good for you to have something to occupy you because when I get my own command I'll be away and that's another reason not to wait.'

Victoria felt as if she'd spoiled this precious moment, but she made up for it later that night when they were in bed together.

When they returned to Southampton they took a taxi to the Langford Hotel to pass on their news to a delighted Lily and Luke, who were thrilled and broke out a bottle of champagne to celebrate.

Lily hugged her daughter. 'I'm so very happy for you, darling. Bruce is perfect for you; I know you'll be very happy with him. He's such a lovely man.'

The next day, Bruce picked Victoria up at her flat and took her to Parkhouse and Wyatt, the jewellers, where she chose a half hoop of emerald and diamonds.

Holding out her hand she was delighted as the diamonds sparkled under the shop lights.

'Oh, Bruce, it's lovely. Thank you.'

'Are you sure it's the one that you really like?'

She assured him that it was and reluctantly took it off for the assistant to place it in the small velvet box.

Later, in her flat, Bruce took the ring from the box and placed it on her finger and kissed her. 'There, now it's official.'

They sat and had a quick sandwich and a cup of coffee when Bruce looked at his watch.

'I'm sorry, darling, but I've got to rush back to the office. I'll come to the club tonight and we'll have dinner together. Come on, I'll drop you off.'

Having arrived, the first person Victoria encountered at the club was Sandy, sitting reading the paper whilst drinking a cup of coffee. He looked up and grinned broadly at her.

'Nice weekend?'

She nodded and asked the waiter to bring more coffee, then she sat beside her old friend. 'I had a lovely time thanks.'

He studied her face. 'Well, darling, you certainly look wonderful. Good sex is always a tonic I always say!'

She slapped him playfully. 'Now don't be naughty!'

Sandy caught hold of her left hand. 'Well! It *was* a good weekend. Congratulations! What a fabulous ring! Hey, George, come and see what Victoria is wearing.'

George Coleman walked over and Sandy held up Victoria's hand. 'Take a look at this!'

Coleman saw the ring and smiled broadly. 'How marvellous! I always hoped you'd end up with Captain Chapman, he's a fine fellow, I'm sure you'll be very happy.' He leaned forward and kissed her cheek.

Victoria finished her coffee then went to her office to catch up on the paperwork that needed her attention. That evening there was a large business party to be catered for in the dining room and Victoria was kept busy for some time, so she didn't see Johnny Daniels arrive. Nor did she see George Coleman walk over to him.

'Miss Teglia got herself engaged this weekend in London,' he told him, 'so any plans you had for making a move on her, young man, have just gone down the tubes!' He walked away grinning to himself.

Johnny was devastated. Just then, Victoria emerged from the dining room and he looked at her left hand and saw the ring she was wearing.

He walked over to her, picked up her hand and angrily asked, 'How could you do such a thing? He's not the man for you and you know it!'

Before she could speak, he caught hold of the back of her head by her hair and kissed her roughly, almost bruising her lips as he did so. Then he walked out of the club.

Eleven

Victoria was stunned. She had been surprised to see Johnny striding towards her and even more surprised by his reaction. It was the ferocity in him that had shocked her. Her head felt sore from his grip and her mouth tender from the onslaught of his kiss.

George hurried over having seen what had happened. 'Are you all right?'

'Yes, yes, honestly.'

'I'll bar him from the club,' George declared. 'He can't behave like that and get away with it!'

'No, don't do that,' Victoria said quickly. 'He'll soon get used to the idea that I'm engaged; let's not make a mountain out of a molehill.'

'Are you sure about this?' Coleman was not happy.

'Yes, I mean it.'

He walked away, convinced she'd made a big mistake. Young Daniels didn't like to lose, and he felt sure the young man wouldn't stand by and do nothing. As far as he was concerned, Daniels was besotted with her and that wasn't a good thing, especially now she was engaged to another man. He'd watch the young shaver closely in future.

Johnny was outside sitting in his car, fuming. He was so sure that Victoria Teglia had feelings for him; he knew the way she responded to his kisses. Was she running scared? Was that why she'd got herself engaged? Jesus! He'd cut himself off from his family for her, for God's sake! He puffed on his cigarette and thought. He knew women and he was certain that, handled with care, he could change things – given time. This was the first woman of the many he'd know that he really wanted – and she *would* be his. About that, he was determined.

★   ★   ★

Pat Daniels was on a train headed for Scotland with a couple of his henchmen. The Scottish laird had not come up with the cash that was due and Daniels wasn't having it. It would be the money or the books – and a chastisement into the bargain. No one treated him this way and got away with it.

The train drew into Edinburgh station and the men alighted. Through his underworld connections, Pat knew there would be a white van waiting for him in a nearby garage, filled with illegal petrol, enough for his needs. He carried a bag and placed it in the back of the van, then, armed with a map, drove out of the city.

It was dark when they arrived at their destination. There were no street lights here to show the way, which suited their plans of arriving unseen. They drove slowly and quietly up a long drive, parking the van in a shrubbery well hidden from view, and crept towards the castle, its turrets visible against the sky when the moon appeared suddenly from behind a cloud.

From the bag, Pat withdrew a couple of baseball bats he'd purloined from the Americans during the war, handed them to his men, then, taking a handgun, he loaded it before they set off towards the building.

There were no curtains drawn at the windows and so they were able to see inside those rooms that were lit. The men crept along and carefully peered into them all, trying to famil-iarize themselves with the layout of the interior. Sitting at the table, in what was obviously the dining room, was the man they were looking for and a woman, both drinking coffee. The men then crept around the back of the building to look for a way in and arrived at the door leading to the kitchen. Through a small window they could observe three members of staff who were clearing away the remnants of the evening meal and obviously preparing to leave the building. The men hid themselves and waited.

About an hour later the staff left, chatting away together, climbing on bicycles left by the wall, unaware they were being watched. When they were well down the drive, the men made for the kitchen door which was still unlocked and let them-selves inside, closing the door quietly behind them.

On the wall was a series of bells, each marked with the name of the room each bell served. Pat nodded to his men and they all quietly left the kitchen, keeping close to the walls, and made their way towards a room where the beam of light under the door was visible and where they heard voices.

Suddenly the door opened and the men dived for cover into a nearby alcove.

'I'm going up now, I'm tired. You come when you're ready,' a female voice said. The men heard footsteps going away from them towards what they hoped were the stairs. Then there was silence.

Pat waited, then stepped out from the alcove, looked around and, nodding to his men, made his way to the room and the door, which was now ajar. He pushed it open just a fraction to allow him to look inside. Sitting in an easy chair by the fire was the laird, smoking his pipe and reading a paper. Pat stepped silently inside, his men following behind and closing the door.

Taking the revolver from his coat pocket, Pat spoke. 'Good evening.'

With a startled look, the Scotsman turned round. 'What the . . .' He stopped mid-sentence when he saw the raised gun.

'I've come for my money!' declared Pat. 'I told you I would, I gave you time to pay and you chose to ignore me. Very foolish, very foolish.'

Donald MacCulloch stared at the weapon. 'Don't be stupid, man!'

'It's you who has been stupid! Did you honestly think you could welch on me?' Pat was livid.

The man went to rise.

'Sit still!'

He did as he was told. 'You can have your money,' he spluttered.

'Do you have it in the house?' asked Daniels.

'Och no, do you think I keep that much money lying about?'

'But no doubt the books are in the library?' Pat had seen such a room listed above one of the bells in the kitchen.

The man looked watchful. 'No, they're not there.'

You're lying, thought the Londoner. 'Let's go take a look

shall we? And don't get clever or believe me I'll blow your bloody brains out!'

The menace in his voice was such that the other man rose carefully from his chair and walked towards the door.

'Don't think of calling for your wife either, not unless you want to have to arrange a funeral.'

The laird led them into a room lined with bookcases filled with books and with a look of triumph said, 'Well, here's the library.'

Daniels saw the look and smirked. 'You think we are an ignorant shower who have no idea about such treasures, don't you? Well let me tell you something you arrogant bastard, these men are probably as knowledgeable as you. They specialize in antique books, that's why we're so successful. We all have our own special field.' He nodded to his men, who started searching the bookshelves. Meantime, Pat pushed his victim into a chair, holding the revolver to his head.

Half an hour later, they found what they were looking for and removed two books.

'But I've already paid you half the money for those!' argued MacCulloch.

'Of course you have, but you were late coming up with the rest of the money so these will cover the interest on the late payment.' Pat laughed at the angry expression on the other man's face.

'Find anything else?' he asked one of his men.

'Yes, guv, another first edition.'

Pat looked at the book and then the fireplace. He threw a lighter at the man and said, 'You know what to do.'

The laird let out a cry of anguish as he realized what was about to happen. Daniels cuffed him round the head with the butt of his gun. 'Shut up!' Blood trickled down the man's cheek.

'You can't destroy that book, it would be sacrilege!' the Scot cried.

'Really?' Pat nodded to his man who held the book open, flicked the lighter and held it to the pages, watching them burn, then he threw it into the fireplace until all that was left was the smouldering cover.

'I'll make you pay for this, Daniels,' MacCulloch threatened.

The villain laughed. 'What you going to do, call the police and report a burglary of stolen goods? I don't think so.'

Donald MacCulloch's expression was filled with hatred. 'For you, all this is just about money! You know the cost of every-thing and the value of nothing.' He glanced into the fireplace at his ruined book then back at Daniels. 'I pity you.'

'You, pity me?' Pat looked at him and grinned. 'Don't you come the high and mighty with me! You are prepared to break the law to accumulate this precious collection. That makes you just as much a villain as I am. The only difference between us is you're an educated man with inherited wealth. But that's not enough for you, is it? No, you're a greedy man. Not content with what you have, you want even more! Which one of us should really be pitied?' I know what I am, but you . . .' He looked round at the paintings of the man's ancestors. 'You besmirch their name!'

His men were getting restless and one of them spoke. 'We should go, guv.'

Daniels glanced at his watch, then turned to his victim. 'You make sure you keep your mouth tightly shut or I'll come back and, next time, I'll burn down your bloody castle!' He strode from the room followed by his two men.

They quickly walked to the van, climbed in and drove away.

'Do you think he'll keep shtum?' asked one.

'What choice does he have?' Daniels laughed. 'Would you, in his position, let the police know you've been buying books that were stolen? Of course not. No, we've nothing to concern ourselves about on that score.'

'What will you do with the two books?' asked the other.

'We'll hang on to them until we find another buyer. We're on a win–win situation. We have half the money he paid us and the books which we can resell. Not bad when you think about it!' Daniels smiled to himself, satisfied with the night's work.

Sandy was coming to the end of his week's holiday. He'd so enjoyed being back in Southampton and realized just how much the place meant to him. Now he'd decided to move back as soon as possible. He'd found a couple of flats that were for rent if his plan materialized. Not in the upmarket part of town, oh no, that wasn't for him at all. He needed to be around the dock area, the places he was familiar with, where he felt at home. He wandered into The Lord Roberts in Canal Walk. It was one of the pubs in which, in the bad old days, Lily used to sing and he played the piano. He ordered a half of bitter and stood talking to the barman.

The bar became busy and Sandy moved over to a small table. Nearby, two men sat drinking. They were dressed in grey utility suits, but even so, they looked a little coarse and rough. Bet they're up to no good, Sandy thought to himself as he finished his drink and left the pub.

He walked back towards Bernard Street and the club. He stopped off at a small cafe and had a sandwich and a cup of coffee. He didn't want to bother Victoria's chef who would be busy with the lunchtime trade. He'd have a snooze this afternoon, ready for his last night, before returning to London in the morning. He'd pop along and see Lily and Luke before he left.

But sitting in the bar of the club later that evening, his plans changed. To his great surprise, the two men he'd seen in The Lord Roberts earlier in the day now wandered into the bar and asked to speak to the owner.

Sandy's eyes narrowed as he watched them. He knew that tonight was George Coleman's night off, which was a worry because he was sure that these two were trouble. He heard the barman telling the men that Miss Teglia would be there in a little while and the men said they would wait and sat down, eyeing up the place with great interest. Quickly, Sandy made his way to Victoria's office, praying the door wouldn't be locked. He let out a sigh of relief when he turned the handle and the door opened. He walked over to the telephone and picked up the receiver.

Fifteen minutes later, Victoria entered the front door and was waylaid by the barman who pointed to the two men. She walked over to them. They both stood up.

'Good evening gentlemen, you wanted to see me?'

'Nice place you have here,' said one of them.

Victoria eyed them suspiciously. 'What can I do for you?'

The taller of the two took over. 'We've heard how well this club is doing,' he said, 'but in this part of town aren't you worried that you might have some trouble?'

'I have a doorman who looks after that for me, thank you.' She eyed them up and down. 'I'm rather surprised he let you in,' she sharply remarked. 'I trust you're not hoping to become members?'

'Now Miss Teglia, that's not very friendly when we are here to offer our services.'

'What can you offer me that I could possibly want?' she asked coldly.

'Protection, that's our business. We make sure that no one who's undesirable bothers you.'

'That won't be necessary, gentlemen, thank you.' Johnny Daniels stood beside Victoria and placed an arm around her shoulders. 'I have Miss Teglia's well being in hand and that of her club. My name is Johnny Daniels, Pat Daniels' son. I'm sure the name is familiar to you both.'

Their attitude changed immediately.

'Right, sorry, Miss Teglia, it seems that we have been misinformed. We won't need to bother you again; we can see you are well taken care of.' They hurried away.

'Johnny! Where did you come from?'

'Sandy called me; he said you may be in trouble. Here, come and sit down, you look a bit pale.' He called for the barman to bring over a brandy. 'Here, drink this.'

At that moment, Sandy walked over. 'You all right, darling?'

She caught hold of his arm. 'Thanks, I wasn't sure quite what was going to happen next. There was no way I would have anything to do with those two. Who the hell are they?'

'I'm not sure,' said Johnny, 'but I aim to find out.'

Victoria looked concerned. 'Please, don't. I can't thank you enough for stepping in like that.' She smiled ruefully. 'Wouldn't you know that it was the night that George wasn't here?'

'That was the idea, I expect,' said Johnny. 'This call was planned.' He shook his head. 'I need to know who is behind this. I've never seen either of them before.'

'Please don't get involved, Johnny,' she pleaded. 'You said you had no part of that kind of life, don't start now.'

He smiled softly at her. 'I do believe you care a little, Victoria, and that makes me very happy.'

She looked at him and realized that she did care – perhaps a little too much.

Twelve

Johnny stayed with Victoria for the rest of the evening. She had been shaken by the visitation of the two thugs. Not for one moment had she even thought that such an encounter might have occurred inside her club. Yes, Bernard Street was not the most salubrious part of town but it had been the site of the old club and times had changed . . . or so she thought, but what had her mother said about people crawling out of the woodwork? It appeared she was correct in her assumption, but, until now, all had been well.

The doorman explained that the two men had said they had business with her which was why he'd allowed them to enter the building.

'I did keep an eye on them, Miss Teglia, but they just sat down quietly and waited for you, so I wasn't too worried at the time. Then you arrived.'

'It's all right,' she assured him, 'they won't be calling again, but if you should see them hanging about . . .'

'Don't you fret miss; I'll soon send them on their way.'

Johnny sat listening to his explanation but said nothing. He knew of the various villains in the area through his background, but these had taken him by surprise. He hadn't heard of any protection racket being run here and he wondered if someone new had moved in. Well, he'd make it his business to find out. He'd have to do this on his own because there was no way he'd ask his father for information. Besides, there was someone he knew in Southampton who'd once dealt with his father who would know all about the local gangs. In a dockland there were always those who could make a living through nefarious ways. Those who, now the war was over, would have to look for new means to supplement their income.

The next morning, Johnny made his way to a small tailor's shop near the Ditches, hidden away in a dingy back street. The bell above the door tinkled as he entered. An elderly rotund man with stooped shoulders walked out of the back room and peered at Johnny over his glasses, perched on the end of a slightly hooked nose.

'Good morning, Solly.'

'My life . . . its young Johnny Daniels, isn't it?'

Johnny chuckled and held out his hand. 'How are you, you old devil? It's been a while.'

The tailor took his hand and shook it. Then he stroked the material of Johnny's suit. 'Nice bit of schmatte.'

Laughing, Johnny said, 'You never change.'

Solly looked him up and down. 'I see you have a decent tailor, you should have come to me. I heard you were in town now. How's business? Here, sit down, sit down.' He removed a bale of cloth from a chair and then sat on one opposite.

'Business is fine, thanks. You still making a fortune?'

The old man looked at him through narrowed eyes. 'What do you really want, eh? You didn't come here to ask about my health; in fact I thought you might have called before now, to look up an old friend, maybe?'

Johnny took out a cigarette and lit it. 'Nothing gets past you, Solly.' He then told him about Victoria and the club and about the two men who had called on her the previous night. 'I want to know who they work for.'

With a sly smile, the tailor gazed at his visitor. 'Yeah, I've heard about the daughter of The Maltese. A looker, I'm told. You got the hots for her, Johnny?'

'Now then, old man,' Johnny chided, 'that's got nothing to do with you, I just want to know what's going on.'

Solly sat back in his chair, undoing his waistcoat which was more than a little tight around his ample girth. 'You're not the only newcomer in town, Johnny boy. About a month ago, some man called Max Reynolds moved in. Nobody knows much about him. He opened up a house-clearance and furniture-removal business. In the Chapel area he has his office. Apparently he's a tough bugger and the men working for him aren't much better. His game? I don't know, but he's made a few waves around town. Upset a few villains, so I hear.'

'In what way?'

'Making his presence felt around the pubs, lording it up a bit from all accounts. But a move he hasn't made as yet . . . unless at the Club Valletta last night, he did?'

Johnny described the two men, then added, 'Make a few enquiries, Solly. If these men are his, give me a ring, will you?' He handed him his business card.

Solly looked at it. 'In the same business as your father, I see. How is Pat these days?'

'Same as ever,' Johnny replied, 'but I'm on my own now, making an honest living.'

The old man raised his eyebrows in surprise. 'Is it straight you're going, my boy?'

'Yes, Solly, I am. I don't want any more of that kind of life. Dad can't understand me, but I'm not him. I am my own man.'

'Then why are you getting involved with Reynolds?'

'I'm trying to safeguard Miss Teglia, that's all.'

With twinkling eyes, Solly smiled. 'Ain't love grand! I'll do what I can and next time you need a suit you come to me, I give you a good price.'

Laughing, Johnny rose to his feet, shook the other man's hand and left the shop. But he frowned as he walked along Canal Walk. The last thing he wanted was to be involved with any gang, but he'd thrown down the gauntlet and he knew that wouldn't please whoever was behind the protection racket. Things wouldn't end there.

In the office of Reynolds Removals, Max Reynolds was listening to the two men who'd visited the Club Valletta and were regaling him about their encounter with the son of Pat Daniels.

Reynolds looked angry. 'I didn't know that Daniels' son was in the area. What's he like?'

'Smart, good looking, and from the way he spoke I'd say he and the Teglia girl have a connection,' said one of the men.

The other man chipped in. 'We don't want to mess with the old man, boss, he's bad news.'

'I'm not having any young whippersnapper telling me what I can and can't do!' retorted Reynolds.

'If we leave the club alone, I don't think he'll bother us,' said the first man. 'We don't want to go looking for trouble, do we? After all, we haven't got established here yet.'

Reynolds gave this some thought. 'All right, we'll leave the club for the moment and see what happens. I've got other plans lined up. But if young Daniels tries to interfere with my business, then he'll be in trouble. I'm not scared of him or his father!'

Victoria had told Sandy not to tell her mother or Luke what had taken place. 'They'll only worry,' she told him. 'Besides, Johnny sorted it out and I'm sure they won't come calling again.'

But she hadn't mentioned Bruce and when he came to the club the following evening and he and Sandy sat having a quiet drink, Sandy told him what had happened.

Seeing the look of concern on the captain's face, Sandy tried to reassure him. 'Don't you worry, Bruce. I rang Johnny Daniels and he came round in a flash and sorted it.'

'What do you mean, sorted it?' Bruce asked sharply.

Sandy told him what Johnny had said.

'And why should the mention of his father frighten these men away?'

It was then that Sandy realized that Bruce knew nothing of Daniels' background, but now he had no choice but to tell him.

Bruce looked appalled as he listened to the facts. 'Whatever is Victoria thinking of allowing him here as a member and, even worse, going out to lunch with him as she did some time ago?'

'Well, to be honest, Bruce, I don't think Johnny has any part of his father's life.'

'Come on, Sandy! How can he live with a villain and not have been involved? You can't be that naive!'

June Tate

'I'm not saying he hasn't got a past, but I do believe he's now making an honest living. This is the first time he's set up his own business and by all accounts he's doing well and people like him.' Sandy put to the back of his mind his suspicions when he saw Johnny and his father plotting together a while back. He liked Johnny and was prepared to give the boy the benefit of the doubt.

But Bruce was furious. 'I can't have Victoria getting mixed up with him; God knows where that could lead. I'll have a word with her later.'

Sandy cursed quietly. This was the last thing he wanted and he wished he'd kept his mouth shut, but now it was too late and as he watched Bruce and Victoria leave the club he wondered just what the outcome would be.

Bruce didn't broach the subject as they drove to the Bellmore Hotel, where they settled down at a table for a quiet drink. He told her his news, that very soon now he hoped to be given his own vessel.

Victoria was delighted for him, knowing how much he missed being at sea. 'Will you be away for any length of time?' she asked.

'Not at first, we'll just be on manoeuvres for a while, so we'll still be able to see one another.'

'And after?'

He didn't want to tell her that he might be sent to Malta for several months as he had hoped she might agree to marry him before that and accompany him, at least for some of the time.

'I don't know, darling, it all depends on the navy. So how are things with you?'

'Fine. We're reasonably busy, most of the rooms are booked and the lunchtime trade is healthy – and of course we're busy at the weekends, so I've no complaints.'

'And that's it?'

Puzzled by the tone of his voice she said, 'That's it. Why do you ask?'

'You didn't think to tell me about the two men who called on you demanding money for protection?'

Victoria realized that Sandy had been talking. 'It was nothing to worry about.'

'What do you mean, nothing? That's demanding money with menaces, it's against the law! Did you report it to the police?'

She saw the anger in his eyes. 'I didn't want the police involved, it's bad for business. Anyway the whole thing was sorted out then and there.'

'By Johnny Daniels, so I'm told. And that's another thing you've kept from me, Victoria: this man's past! For Christ's sake, we are engaged; shouldn't you be sharing all this with me?'

'Johnny's past is his own business and not anyone else's, certainly not yours!' Now her face was flushed with anger.

'It damned well is my business when he's around you. You've even been out to lunch with him and consorting with a criminal is not good for you or the business you're so concerned about!'

'Johnny Daniels is *not* a criminal!'

Bruce lowered his voice. 'Are you absolutely sure about that, Victoria?'

She hesitated for just a moment. 'Yes, I am.'

Bruce sipped his drink, gazing at her over the rim of the glass. 'You're not sure at all. Darling, I know you so well, so please don't pretend with me.'

She didn't answer, what could she say? She wanted to believe that Johnny was leading a life without crime, but he'd used his father as a threat to the two men who'd been in the club. A threat that had the desired effect. She was now confused.

Bruce leaned forward. 'Look, darling, I'm just concerned for you because I love you, but I have to be honest, this thing between you and Daniels worries me.'

'What on earth do you mean . . . this thing?'

'It's as if he has some kind of hold over you.' He shrugged. 'I don't know what it is but when I see you together . . . like the time he came over to us when we were dining at the Cowherds. He did that deliberately. Why?'

'I have no idea!' she exclaimed.

'Well maybe I should ask him.'

'You can't do that!' She was shocked at the idea.

'Why ever not? He needs to know that you and I are getting married, that you will be my wife – and that he needs to back off.'

Bruce wasn't easily angered but now she could see that he meant business and, if Bruce tackled Johnny, she wasn't at all sure what he would say, remembering clearly how he took the news of their engagement.

She tried to reason with her fiancé. 'Truly, there's no need for all this, Bruce darling. There's nothing between Johnny Daniels and me. He's just a member, that's all, and Sandy thought I was in trouble and called him.'

'And he couldn't get to you quickly enough! You may not have any feelings for him, but maybe he thinks differently.'

She held out her left hand. 'I'm wearing your ring, aren't I? That should tell you something, I'd have thought.'

Bruce let the matter drop but the rest of the evening was spent with an unspoken atmosphere between them.

When they returned to the club, Bruce didn't go in. He helped Victoria out of the car, held her close and kissed her longingly. 'Remember I love you,' he whispered against her cheek.

'And I love you,' she said and watched him drive away with some relief. That had been a difficult evening, she thought as she stepped through the club door. The first person she saw sitting at the bar, smiling at her, was Johnny Daniels.

Thirteen

'Hello, gorgeous!' said Johnny, kissing her cheek. 'I thought I'd missed you. What would you like to drink?'

'Nothing thanks,' she said, 'I've got a lot of work to catch up on.'

'How's the captain?' he asked quietly. 'Only, the barman told me you were with him when I asked after you.'

Victoria looked at Johnny, asking herself exactly what was

the hold he had over her. Was it purely sexual? He only had to smile at her and she seemed to be under some kind of spell. She longed for him to reach out and touch her, and, in unguarded moments, wondered what it would be like to be made love to by this handsome but dangerous man. The idea excited her and whenever she told herself the whole idea was more than foolish, it didn't make a bit of difference. Perhaps the only way to lay this ghost to rest was to find out.

'He's fine, thanks, but he's not too happy about you being around.'

Johnny found this most amusing. 'I bet he isn't!'

'What on earth do you mean?'

He took her hand and stroked it with his thumb. 'He knows that I want you, it's as simple as that.'

His touch, though gentle seemed to imprint every movement on her skin. 'Do you want me, Johnny?'

His gaze never left her face. 'Oh yes.'

She held his gaze for a long time, battling with her emotions, making choices, wondering just what to do. Then, quietly, she spoke.

'Well, let's go.'

He didn't answer but just rose from his seat still holding her hand and led her out of the building. They drove in silence and, when they reached his flat, he led her to the door, opened it and then without hesitation, took her into the bedroom.

'Come here,' he said as he took her into his arms and kissed her.

Victoria lost herself in the moment, returning his kisses with mounting passion until they were both breathless. He slowly undressed her, kissing and caressing parts of her lithe body as he threw each garment aside until she was naked in his arms.

'You are even more beautiful than I ever imagined,' he told her as he cupped her breast in his hand, running his thumb over her now pert nipple.

She moaned quietly as he laid her on the bed, swiftly took off his own clothes and then proceeded to tease her with his deft fingers and mouth, until her senses were swimming.

When eventually he was on top of her, she was ready for him and forgot about everything else, enjoying every thrust of his strong body until they lay replete and exhausted in each other's arms.

Johnny said not a word as he held her close, caressing her gently, kissing her softly until they both fell asleep.

Victoria was the first to wake. She stirred then opened her eyes. Johnny's arms were holding her close and she turned her head and studied the face next to hers on the pillow. No one had made her feel like that during love making, not even Bruce, who knew her body so well. She felt a stab of guilt. She shouldn't be here, after all she was wearing Bruce's ring, had promised to marry him. Earlier she was convinced the only way to cure herself of Johnny Daniels was to be with him just once – and then he'd be out of her system, but in fact it had only made matters worse.

She ran her finger softly over his mouth, the same mouth that had given her so much pleasure. His eyelids fluttered then he opened his eyes . . . and smiled.

'Hello,' he said softly and, gathering her even closer, kissed her, slowly. Then he slipped his hand between her thighs . . .

The same night, Max Reynolds and some of his men broke into the warehouse where Johnny Daniels kept the tools of his trade and his work vehicles and slashed the tyres and window screens of the three vans parked there.

'Just a small lesson for Mr Daniels to teach him not to interfere in my business,' Max remarked as he was driven away. 'He needs to know I'm not a man to be messed with – whoever his father might be!'

In the morning Johnny was about to enter his office whistling happily only to be stopped by one of his men.

'You'd better come with me, Mr Daniels,' he said.

Something in the tone of the man's voice made Johnny cease his whistling and follow him to the warehouse, where he saw the damaged tyres and smashed screens.

'Who would do a thing like this?' his man demanded. 'And why?'

Without answering, Johnny turned on his heel, walked

quickly to his car and drove to the Chapel area where he found the office of Max Reynolds and, pushing the door open, walked in.

Reynolds was sitting behind a large desk. He looked up, saw his visitor and smiled.

'Johnny Daniels, I presume,' he said mockingly

'What's your point, Reynolds?' asked Johnny without preamble.

'Don't interfere in my business, son. That's my point!' He sat back in his chair and stared at the young man in front of him.' And don't threaten me with your father, it won't wash!'

Johnny remained calm. 'I don't give a shit what you get up to in this town, Reynolds, but you leave the Club Valletta alone! That's *my* point.'

'You got it made with the daughter of The Maltese, is that it?'

'Miss Teglia is none of your business; you just keep your hoods away from her and her business.'

'Or what?'

'Let's not go there. I'm sure you don't want trouble, it only brings in the coppers and you wouldn't want that, would you?'

Reynolds didn't like being told what to do but at the same time he wasn't looking for trouble either. The two men glared at each other for a minute, then Johnny walked out of the office, fuming. If he was still part of his father's operation, this incident would have been dealt with gangland fashion, but he wanted to put that world behind him, so he walked away, which really stuck in his craw and put him in a bad mood for the rest of the day as he paid for repairs to his vehicles. Which, in this day and age, was no mean feat . . . and expensive.

Whilst all this was going on, in London, Pat Daniels was planning his next job in Southampton. The house in Romsey, according to his son, housed some priceless antiques, which was manna from heaven as far as old man Daniels was concerned. There was a ready market for such things and he had the buyers lined up, waiting, which meant he didn't have to keep the goods for long, which was a much safer bet. Unlike the books he'd retrieved from the Scottish Laird, which were still hidden in his warehouse.

He instructed his men to go down to Southampton and find a cheap bed and breakfast and then visit Romsey to find out what they could about the house in question.

'Whatever you do, don't stay in Romsey itself, it's too small a place, people will notice strangers who are around too long. Day trippers go there all the time, so then you'll blend in with them.'

After they'd left, Pat considered his son's reaction if he managed to pull the job, but Johnny would just have to get on with it. He'd made it clear that he was now on his own so there would be no more useful information coming from him and this was too good an opportunity to be missed.

When she left Johnny's flat, Victoria went to her own and had a bath and changed, ready for work. She found herself humming and smiling as she dressed. This was madness! She tried to collect her thoughts, but all she could think about was the feel of Johnny Daniels, the scent of him, his mouth on hers, his hands as he'd caressed her, the thrill she felt as they made love – and she realized she had to decide what to do. This wasn't fair on Bruce. He was an honourable man who loved her, he didn't deserve to be treated so badly and now she felt really guilty. But she knew in her heart she wasn't ready to settle down and it was only right that Bruce should be told. She picked up the telephone and dialled his number.

'Hello, Bruce, can you come round to the flat this evening? I need to talk to you.'

On the other end of the line, Bruce Chapman frowned. Knowing Victoria as well as he did, he knew that this was serious and, for some unknown reason, he guessed that this was about their future.

'Yes, darling, of course, what time?'

'Severn thirty?'

'Yes, that's fine. Are you all right, Victoria?'

She hesitated. 'I just need to talk to you.'

His heart sank. 'Very well, I'll see you later.'

When Victoria eventually arrived at the club, she found Sandy, suitcase by his side, reading the paper and drinking coffee. He looked up as she walked in.

'I'm going back to the smoke today, darling, got time to have a coffee with me before I go?' he asked.

She sat beside him and asked a waiter to bring another pot of coffee over. 'Are you coming back to live here after all?' she asked.

'Yes, I am. I have rented a small flat for the time being. I need to tidy up some things before I finally move, but yes, I'm coming home.' He stared at her. 'What's the matter?'

With a look of surprise she said, 'Matter? What makes you think something's wrong?'

'Darling child, I've watched you grow, I know all your expressions and now you've got something on your mind. Want to talk it over with an old and trusted friend?'

She let out a sigh of relief. Sandy had always been in her life and he was just the person she needed right now.

'I'm going to break off my engagement tonight and I feel an absolute bitch!'

He took out a cigarette and lit it slowly. 'Johnny Daniels got under your skin then?'

Her eyes widened with surprise. 'Is it so obvious?'

'Only to people who know you really well. Are you sure you're making the right choice?'

She pushed her fingers through her hair with frustration. 'No, I'm not! All I know is that I'm not being fair to Bruce. How can I wear his ring and want another man?'

'You can't! But what if this is just infatuation – or just plain lust? You will have ruined your happiness with a good man.'

'I know! But I have to be truthful with Bruce or I couldn't live with myself.' She hesitated. 'You know Johnny. Am I being a complete fool?'

Sandy was at a loss. He liked young Daniels, he also knew his record with women, but he also felt that Victoria meant more to him than was usual. Yet . . . his background made Sandy somewhat wary.

'To be honest, darling, I don't know. This is something only you can sort out and, as they say, only time will tell. I just hope you don't get hurt in the process.'

'Poor Bruce is the one who will be hurt and it's all my fault!'

Sandy's taxi arrived at that moment and Victoria reluctantly saw him off the premises.

'I'll be back very soon,' he told her, 'and we'll talk again. But be kind to Bruce when you tell him, that man adores you.' He kissed her goodbye and was driven away.

That evening, Victoria was pacing up and down in her flat, awaiting Bruce's arrival. Her nerves were in tatters. Bruce had meant something very special in her life. When they'd been together in France, they'd been very close as lovers and as friends and she didn't know quite how she was going to tell him her news. Whichever way she had rehearsed, she couldn't find the right words and the more she tried the worse it became. The front-door bell rang and with her heart pounding, she opened the door.

'Hello, darling.' He stepped inside and gave her a bottle of wine. 'I think we are both going to need a drink, don't you?' He kissed her on her cheek. 'Find me a corkscrew and then we'll talk.'

He opened the bottle, filled two glasses, gave her one then, taking her by the other hand, led her to the settee.

'Right, now, what's this all about?'

'I'm sorry, Bruce, but I can't marry you.' She hadn't meant to blurt it out quite so suddenly but the words just tumbled out of her mouth. She looked at him with tears in her eyes.

'I see.' He sipped slowly from his glass. 'Has this anything to do with Johnny Daniels?'

She nodded, at a loss for words for a moment. 'I am *so* sorry, Bruce. I feel dreadful about letting you down, but I can't wear your ring any longer feeling as I do.' She picked up the little box on the table and handed it to him. 'I do hope you can forgive me.'

For a moment he was silent. 'I have to say this is not a complete surprise, Victoria. If I'm honest I have seen it coming. But, darling, don't throw away our happiness for him, he's really not worth it!'

She was immediately defensive. 'How can you say such a thing?'

'Because I have dealt with men all my adult life. His type will always let you down.'

'People can change!' Her face was flushed with anger. 'I know he comes from a dodgy background, but he works hard and is in a legitimate business now.'

'And you are obsessed with him! He's always hanging around, no doubt working his charm on you and you've fallen for it. Oh, Victoria, I thought you had more sense.'

'Don't treat me like a child, Bruce, because I'm not one. I'm very much a grown woman!'

'Of course you are, but you're also vulnerable. This man is temptation personified. He must seem exciting to you especially because of his background . . . or is there more to it than that?'

'What do you mean?'

'Have you slept with him?' He looked steadily at her and she didn't answer. 'I see.' His words were clipped and angry.

'I am so sorry, Bruce. I thought it would get him out of my system if I did.'

'You didn't think to say no, I'm sorry, but I'm engaged and in love with another man?' Now he was furious.

She just shook her head.

Bruce rose to his feet. 'There's nothing more to be said, except that I am truly disappointed in you, Victoria. I trusted you implicitly, I wanted to spend the rest of my life with you, you meant that much to me, but obviously I wasn't that important to you.' He threw the box with the ring in it on to the coffee table.

As he walked out of the door, Victoria just watched in silence. After all, what could she say? Then as the door closed behind him, she burst into tears.

Fourteen

Bruce made his way to the Langford Hotel, walked into the bar and asked for a large whiskey and soda. He sat deep in thought, unaware that Lily, Victoria's mother was approaching.

'Hello, Bruce, how's my future son-in-law?' She kissed his cheek and sat beside him.

'Let me get you a drink, Lily, you can join me as I get smashed.'

'Why, whatever is the matter?'

'Victoria broke our engagement this evening.'

'What? Whatever are you talking about?'

He smiled wryly. 'She's fallen for Johnny Daniels it would seem.'

Lily looked puzzled. 'Say that again.'

'I know, I could hardly believe it either.' He rubbed his forehead wearily. 'I don't know what to do. I really love her, Lily, and she's making a dreadful mistake and nothing I can say will change that.'

'Oh, Bruce, I am so sorry.'

'Maybe she'll come to her senses in time, but it'll be too late for us.' He took a long drink from his glass.

'What are you going to do?' she asked anxiously.

'Sail off into the sunset! Next week I'm being given my own vessel and we're off for manoeuvres. Perfect timing, don't you think?'

She heard the bitterness in his voice and was sad. She so admired this man and had thought him a perfect husband for Victoria. Now she was worried. Victoria was stubborn and wayward. Johnny Daniels was a charmer and had a way with women, she'd seen that for herself and Victoria had fallen for his charms it would seem. She was throwing her future away . . . for what?

'Is there anything I can do, Bruce?'

He shook his head. 'No, but thanks for asking. You know as well as I do that once Victoria has decided on something, she becomes stubborn if anyone tries to change her mind.'

'Yes I'm afraid so, she takes after her father in that way. But on the other hand, she won't suffer fools gladly and if Johnny Daniels plays her up, she'll show him the door.'

'Perhaps, but she liked him enough to sleep with him!'

Lily was shaken. This madness had gone further than she imagined – and so soon. She saw the pain in Bruce's face and her heart went out to him.

'I'm really sorry, Bruce. I don't know what to say.'

He finished his drink, climbed down from the bar stool and kissed her on the cheek. 'There's nothing to be said, sadly. I'm going back to my quarters. I'll be in touch.'

Lily watched him walk away. How could Victoria have been so stupid? She wanted to shake her.

Luke walked in the bar at that moment. 'I thought I saw Bruce leaving just now.'

She told him what had transpired.

'I'm really sorry to hear that,' he said, 'but Lily, you can't interfere, this is between Victoria and Bruce. She isn't a child and she must be allowed to make her own decisions.'

'As if I would!'

'Don't look so outraged, I know you. Leave them alone!'

Luke was called away and Lily sat ruminating over his words. She wanted desperately to call Victoria and remonstrate with her but it would only make matters worse. Luke was right. She left the bar and went to her office, totally deflated.

Victoria, now alone in her flat, was feeling much the same. She'd cried so much after Bruce had gone, she was empty of emotion. She felt so guilty about hurting him after such a close relationship, but really she didn't have a choice.

The telephone rang and she cursed. She didn't feel like talking to anybody, but she had to answer it in case it was from the club. She picked up the receiver. 'Hello.'

'Victoria?' It was Johnny.

'Hello, Johnny.'

'Whatever is the matter, you sound awful?'

'I've just broken off my engagement to a lovely man and I feel dreadful.' The words stuck in her throat.

'I'm coming round now.' She heard him put the receiver down and ten minutes later she opened the door to Johnny Daniels. He stepped inside, closed the door and took her into his arms and held her.

'It'll be all right, you'll see,' he said quietly. 'I'm going to take good care of you, Victoria. I promise.'

She stared into his eyes. 'I've given up a good man for you – you'd better be worth it!'

He started to laugh. 'I love a feisty woman,' he said and kissed her.

In the small town of Romsey, the following morning, life continued as usual for the local inhabitants, going about their business. Visitors milled around, some taking trips to Broadlands, the home of the Mountbattens, and others shopped for souvenirs. Two of Pat Daniels' men were sitting having a coffee, reading the local paper, gleaning any information they could about the area and the occupants of the house they planned to rob in the near future.

The owner, it appeared, came from a wealthy family and worked at Lloyds in London, was well liked, generous to local charities and opened his garden to the public twice a year. In the spring and the late summer and the following Sunday it would be open from eleven o'clock until two. The Londoners couldn't believe their luck. They travelled back to Southampton and enjoyed the next two days visiting as many public houses as possible. On Sunday morning, suffering greatly from drinking far too much alcohol, they waited for a train to take them back to Romsey.

The stately home belonging to Edward Mansfield and his family stood in ten acres of ground, with hidden gardens, artfully laid out in different areas with deep flowerbeds, arbours, and wooden benches that invited you to sit and admire the view at leisure. Now it was ablaze with rhododendrons and azaleas. A woodland flourished, carpeted with bluebells. It was a feast of colour for the eyes, but the two men from London were not in the least bit interested.

They wandered nearer to the house, walking round the rose beds and up the wide steps to inspect the tall, imposing jardinières standing like sentinels at the top, in front of the wide glass windows. Glancing around to see if they were being observed, they sauntered along the building, peering inside the sumptuous rooms eyeing the contents with glee. These men knew about antique furniture – and inside was a small fortune. In a tall, glass-fronted case was a collection of priceless porcelain. But this would not be an easy job. To remove any of the larger objects inside would need a furniture van and some muscle. Hardly unobtrusive, and to do this, the house would not have to be occupied and, from what they were able to observe, Mr Mansfield lived high of the hog and was well attended. The men returned to the town for a hair of the dog at the nearest public house where they discussed their problem.

'There's too many people about,' said one, 'and we've yet to discover their alarm system. I reckon we should give this one the elbow, myself.'

Shrugging, his companion agreed. 'But you know the boss, whatever we think we'll have to find out more detail before we go back to him or we'll be in trouble.'

It seemed that luck was truly on their side that day. As they sat discussing the problem a man came into the bar, dressed in chef's attire beneath his jacket. He walked up to the counter and ordered a half of bitter.

The landlord greeted him warmly. 'Have many visitors to the garden today, chef?'

'Yes, Mr Mansfield will be pleased, his charities should do well out of it. I've got a dinner party tomorrow night and I've just been to collect the meat from the butcher.'

The two Londoners looked at each other and nodded. They casually walked over to the bar. 'Couldn't help overhearing your conversation,' said one. 'We were at the garden this morning. What a marvellous place, must be worth a mint of money. You must be pretty good at your job to work there.'

The chef was flattered. 'Yes, well, I trained in London at some of the top restaurants. I was last at the Savoy.'

The men looked suitably impressed.

'If the house were mine,' said the other, 'I'd be worried sick about being burgled. A home like that must be full of treasures.'

'We don't worry about such things,' the chef told them. 'We have a great alarm system and recently Mr Mansfield installed a brand new one recommended by a friend of his. He had one installed himself. He was told about it by the bloke mending his roof. Young Mr Daniels has done them both a favour.'

He downed the rest of his drink, nodded to them and left the bar.

The two men looked at each other. 'That's put the mockers

on it then. The old man won't be happy, especially when we tell him about young Johnny.'

'Best get back to London,' said his companion. 'There's no point in hanging around.'

When Pat Daniels was given the news, he was livid. 'What the bloody hell is the boy thinking of? The stuff in this place is worth a fortune.'

One of his men interrupted. 'Even so, boss, without the new alarm, it would be pretty impossible. There's far too many people milling about and Mansfield comes back from London most nights from what we could gather. It would be a very risky undertaking.'

Pat was too enraged to listen to reason. 'Every property has a weak spot. It would just take longer to discover it and, from what you tell me, the wait would have been worthwhile. I could throttle the bastard. My own son! How could he do this to me? Well I'm bloody well going to find out!'

The following day was Saturday. Pat had been delayed in London, so when his train drew into Southampton it was early evening. He took a taxi to Johnny's office in the High Street, but it was closed for the weekend, his flat was also unoccupied, so he asked the driver to take him to the Club Valletta where he paid him off. But as he made his way to the entrance, the doorman stopped him.

'Can I help you, sir?'

Pat glowered at him. 'No thanks, I can find my own way.'

The man stepped in front of him, barring the way. 'I don't believe you are a member, sir.'

'No, I've come to see my son who *is* a member!' Daniels snapped.

'And who might that be, sir?'

'Mr Johnny Daniels, now get out of my way!' He tried to push past the man, but the doorman, now quietly enraged by his treatment, took him firmly by the arm.

'Sorry, sir, but I can't let you go in. Mr Daniels has not yet arrived and without him, there's no way I'm letting you inside these premises.'

Hearing the raised voices, George Coleman walked outside

to see what was causing it. He recognized Pat Daniels immediately but he ignored him and turned to the doorman.

'What's going on?'

'This gentleman isn't a member, Mr Coleman, he's looking for young Mr Daniels but he's not here.'

George thought quickly. Although Pat Daniels was well dressed, unlike his son he was a rough diamond and he thought this was a great opportunity for Victoria to see what she was getting herself into. He'd been appalled when he'd heard about her broken engagement and thought that this might just be the very thing to bring her to her senses.

'I'll sign this gentleman in,' he told the doorman, 'but you were right to be so vigilant. You did a good job. Thanks, I'll take it from here.'

Thus mollified, the doorman glared at Daniels and stepped aside.

Pat began to thank George but he interrupted him. 'You'll sign the visitor's book, I'll buy you a drink because only members are allowed to do so, but if your son doesn't arrive in the next thirty minutes, then I'll have to ask you to leave. What do you want?'

Inwardly, Daniels fumed. No one dared speak to him this way on his own home ground, but he swallowed his pride and ordered a pint of beer. When he'd been served, George took him to a seat and told him to wait there, then he walked away. This should be really interesting, he thought, and smiled softly to himself as he waited to see what happened.

Twenty minutes later, Johnny Daniels walked into the club and ordered a drink. He didn't see his father until he felt a tap on his shoulder.

'Hello, son.'

'Dad! What on earth are you doing here?'

Pat's face looked as if it had been carved in granite. 'I need to talk to you.'

'How did you get in here?' asked Johnny. 'They are really strict about non-members.'

'George Coleman let me in.'

This immediately put Johnny on his mettle. George hated him with a vengeance, so he must have some devious reason for his action and, looking at the expression on his father's face, Johnny knew this meeting was not going to be a good one.

'Let's go to a pub, then we can talk,' he suggested.

But Pat wouldn't hear of it. Just to spite Coleman, he was determined to stay. His stubbornness played right into George's hands.

'No, we'll stay here.'

Johnny had no choice but to follow his father and sit down. 'What is it that demands a personal visit?' he asked with some trepidation.

'I hear you've become involved in another business just lately.'

His son frowned. What on earth was he referring to? 'Like what?'

'Newfangled alarm systems – or so I'm told!'

'You've been to Romsey.'

'Then it's true! What the bloody hell do you think you're playing at? How dare you interfere in my business?'

'No, Dad, you've got it wrong, you would be interfering in *my* business! I asked you not to pull any more jobs here and you ignored me, so I had no choice but to protect myself.' Now it was Johnny who was angry. 'Perhaps now you'll leave Southampton out of your schemes.'

'If anyone else but my own son pulled such a flanker . . . well you know how I deal with such people.' Pat was white with anger. 'All because of a bit of bloody skirt!'

George Coleman was watching the scene from a hidden vantage point, enjoying himself because it was obvious the two men were at cross purposes. At that moment Victoria arrived.

Both Daniels saw her at the same time. Pat looked Victoria up and down as she stopped and spoke to the barman. 'Well, I have to say, your taste has improved, but in bed all women are the same if you close your eyes.'

'Don't talk about Victoria like that!' Johnny snapped. 'She's worth some respect, especially from you!'

The barman told Victoria that Johnny was in the club and indicated towards the table where the men sat. She walked over to them, smiling.

'Hello, Johnny, I didn't see you when I came in.' She looked at Pat and smiled. 'Good evening, I don't believe we've met.'

He stood up and shook her hand. 'Hello, Miss Teglia, how nice to meet you. I'm Johnny's father.'

She looked surprised. 'Mr Daniels. You're some way from home, aren't you?'

'The Smoke isn't that far, you should come and visit with us some time.'

She stared at the man, smiling at her, and noted that the smile didn't reach his eyes that were coldly staring back and she knew she didn't like anything about him. Even in a hand-tailored suit he was uncouth. But as she looked at him, a shiver ran down her spine. This man was menacing even as he spoke polite platitudes to her.

'You must excuse me, I have things to see to,' she said and walked quickly away.

Johnny rose to his feet. 'I'll drive you to the station,' he said firmly. Pat had no recourse but to leave, albeit reluctantly.

George found Victoria in her office, lost in thought.

'So, you've met the mighty Daniels. Take it from me, girl, that's one mean bugger and never to be crossed unless you want to invite trouble.'

She looked at her protector. 'I can't believe he's Johnny's father, they are so different.'

'Are you quite certain about that, Victoria? They say acorns don't fall far from the tree. Just be very careful you don't bring a heap of trouble on yourself, that's all.' He walked away and left her with her thoughts, hoping that tonight he'd seen off young Johnny Daniels.

Fifteen

'Just keep out of my life, Dad, and I'll keep out of yours!' had been Johnny's parting shot to his irate father when he dropped him at the train station. He then drove quickly back to the club and enquired as to the whereabouts of Miss Teglia from the barman. He made his way to her office and, knocking briefly on the door, walked in.

'Look I'm sorry about inflicting my father on you like that, but I didn't know he was coming.'

She stared at him without answering, silently comparing the two men. They couldn't have been more different. Johnny's features were not coarse as were his father's, so he must take after his mother, she assumed. His speech was far more refined, too. There had not been an atom of charm about Pat Daniels and she could believe that he was a villain and a man not to be messed with, yet her lover standing before her was his son.

'What did he want that brought him down here? It must have been important.'

'It was about some goods he was expecting, they were delayed and he wondered if I was having the same trouble with the firm. We both deal with the same man – that's all.'

She had the feeling he was lying to her. 'I thought you had nothing to do with him any more – or his business.'

'I don't, but don't forget, Victoria, we are both in the construction game and sometimes it can be difficult to purchase the goods that are vital to our success. It can be a serious problem. One that we share.'

She was not convinced, but what could she say? 'Don't ever think of recommending him for membership, Johnny, because I don't want him on my premises.'

There was an icy tone to her voice and, at that moment, he realized that Victoria was not a woman to be messed with either. He'd really have to watch his step in the future and he cursed his father for making waves in their relationship. But he just smiled.

'Are you crazy? I certainly don't want him around! I've told you he is no longer a part of my life.'

'I wonder if he believes that?' she said and stared hard at him.

'Believe me, I made that perfectly clear when I took him to the station.' He gazed lovingly at her. 'Come on, darling, let's go and have a quiet drink together before you get too busy.'

'Not tonight, I've got some paperwork to do and I need to get on with it.' She picked up a pile of letters and took no further notice of him.

Johnny knew this was not the time to argue. It was obvious

that his father's visit had unsettled her and he could understand why. He would just have to give her time to get over it.

'All right, Victoria, I'll call you tomorrow,' he said and left her alone.

George Coleman watched him walk out of the club with a feeling of great satisfaction. It was obvious that he'd been dismissed as Victoria didn't follow him. Well, that was great. He'd sowed the seed and now waited for it to flourish. Job well done!

Victoria *was* unsettled. Here she was partner of the club on the same site with the same name as her father's club. Her father who had been a renowned villain, she knew that, but it wasn't until she'd met Pat Daniels that the fact became a reality. This was the world and kind of people that Vittorio had been mixed up with and she didn't like it. Was he like the Londoner? God, she hoped not! But she had been told by her mother that he could be ruthless when necessary. How far did he go? Did he ever kill a man? She felt sure that Pat Daniels was capable of murder – just by looking into his eyes. Could Johnny be ruthless too? She remembered his reaction when he first learned she was engaged. The rough way he'd grabbed and kissed her had shocked her. She'd forgotten about it until now – and now she was filled with uncertainty. Had she made a terrible mistake?

Carefully tidying her desk, she put the letters to one side, rose from her chair and left the office. She looked for George and told him she would like to go home for the night, could he manage without her?

'Yes, love, off you go,' he said. 'You look a bit peaky, are you all right?'

'Just a bit tired, that's all. I'll see you in the morning.' And she left.

Pat Daniels was furious when he got on to the London train. He was livid that a very valuable job had been scuppered by his own son and the way George Coleman had shown little or no respect towards him, knowing his reputation. But what really stuck in his craw was Johnny. To think that his own son, who, until he'd come down to Southampton, would never, *never* have crossed him or questioned him in any way and now was telling him to keep out of his life! Who did the little bastard think he was? Well, he needed a lesson. Daniels alighted from the train at the next station.

Max Reynolds was just about to leave his office when he had an unexpected visitor. One of his men came rushing in.

'Boss, boss, Pat Daniels is here to see you!'

Reynolds was shaken when he heard the name. He knew all about the man and wondered what on earth he was doing asking for him. He sat back behind his desk and somewhat nervously told his man to let him in.

With a face like thunder, Pat Daniels marched into the room and sat down, glared at the other man and spoke. 'I've got a job for you!'

Bruce Chapman was getting his papers up to date ready to hand over to the man taking his place. Tomorrow he was due to take over his own command. He couldn't wait to get away. His broken engagement still weighed heavily with him and he still couldn't understand why Victoria was behaving in such a rash manner. It wasn't as if they had been at loggerheads. Quite the opposite. Since he'd been moved to Portsmouth they'd got along together just like they had in France. They'd enjoyed each other's company, their sex life was great as it always had been – then suddenly it was over. Had he seen it coming it would have helped, but her decision came out of the blue and he was still reeling from it if he was honest. Now he couldn't wait to go to sea; there was nothing to keep him here any more.

He picked up a photograph of her mounted in a silver frame and studied it before putting it in his briefcase. That just about covered everything. He took one look around the office then walked away.

The following morning he was driven to the dockyard where a cruiser was anchored and he walked up the gangway. At the top stood an officer waiting to greet him. He saluted smartly.

'Lieutenant Mark Hattfield, sir. Welcome aboard.'

Bruce returned the salute. 'Morning Hattfield. Right, let's take the tour.'

★   ★   ★

Sandy, now all packed and ready to move back to Southampton, was sitting in the Smuggler's Return having a quiet beer with the barman.

'Won't you miss being here, Sandy?'

'No love, to be honest. I've had enough of playing in pubs to last a lifetime. Now I want some me time. I want a bit of fun in my life before I pop my clogs!'

The barman laughed. 'So will you be looking for a nice sailor then?'

Grinning broadly, Sandy laughed. 'Well, I do love a man in uniform, I must say. But really, I'm just tired of my old life and Southampton means a lot to me and I've got some good friends there. I want to be free to spend time with them.'

'You might come across young Daniels, he's got a business there, I believe.'

'Yes, that's more than likely. I haven't seen him in here lately.'

The barman leaned across the bar. 'Rumour has it that he wants to break away from the old man. Can't say I blame him. The boy's cut out for a better life if he's got any sense.'

When the barman left him to serve another customer, Sandy wondered if Johnny had decided to cut his ties with his father after he'd met Victoria. All he needed was a good woman to keep him on the straight and narrow and, liking the fellow as he did, he fervently hoped that was the case. After all, she'd broken her engagement to Bruce for him and he prayed she'd made the right decision.

At that moment Pat Daniels walked into the bar with one of his men.

'Hello, Sandy, I hear you are leaving us,' he said.

'Yes, I'm retiring. I'm going back to Southampton, my old hunting ground. I expect I'll see something of Johnny whilst I'm there.'

The smile disappeared from the other's face. 'That boy forgets where he came from! Since he moved there he's got a bit too big for his boots to my mind. Anyway, I wish you luck. I'll miss you and your entertaining ways. Just keep away from the dockyards.' And he sat down.

Sandy frowned. He hoped that any bad feeling between father and son was not going to affect Victoria in any way.

He'd keep a careful eye on her when he moved, because he knew that Daniels' anger was legendary and it usually meant trouble for someone.

Sixteen

Max Reynolds puffed out his chest as Pat Daniels left his office. Now he was really mixing with the big boys. He was a small-time crook loaded with ambition and now he felt he was really getting somewhere. Big Pat came to him! He went over the details in his mind, trying to plan how when and . . . well, he knew where. The big man's last words rang in his ears.

'No way can this be traced back to me. You do well, I'll take care of you.'

The London mobster would owe him . . . Max Reynolds! Oh, how he wished he could crow about it when he went to the pub, but of course he couldn't. Secrecy was absolute.

Three days later, Victoria walked wearily from the taxi to her door. It had been a very busy night, her feet were killing her and she wanted a bath before climbing into bed. As she was about to put the key in her front door, she realized that it was slightly open and frowned. She knew she'd locked it earlier, but, as you do in such situations, she questioned herself. Had she been in a hurry and not closed it properly? No, she was always so careful. Then she became tense. This really wasn't right. She looked around. The building was silent. At this hour the other tenants would be in their beds, asleep. With her heart thumping, she slowly pushed open the door and groped for the light switch before opening the door further. She gasped at what she saw. The place was a shambles.

Chairs had been tumbled over, table lamps smashed, drawers emptied and the expensive wall mirrors smashed. Her record player was broken as were many of her records. She was shocked. Quickly trying to gather her wits, she knew better than to touch anything. Searching carefully amongst the wreckage she found the telephone, thankfully intact, and rang the police.

She was sitting on the floor outside the door smoking nervously when the police arrived. A constable and a detective entered the block and found her. They took down the details and asked if she had moved or touched anything inside.

'Only the phone, other than that, nothing.'

The two men walked gingerly into the room, stopping just inside the door. After a look round the detective spoke.

'Have you somewhere you can stay tonight, Miss Teglia?'

'Yes,' she said, 'I can go to the Langford Hotel and stay with my mother.' Luke would have to be told as, after all, this was his property.

'I'll leave the constable here, miss, until my men come and look for fingerprints. I'll drive you over there, shall I?'

'Thank you, that would be kind of you. Can I grab some night clothes?'

'Best not; you could mess up the crime scene if you do.'

'Oh yes, of course.'

During the short drive to Cumberland Place, the detective tried to cheer her.

'We'll go over the place with a fine toothcomb for fingerprints and when we've done you can look the place over and see if anything's missing. Don't you worry, we'll find the perpetrators. Can you think of anyone who might have a grudge against you?'

She shook her head. 'No I can't imagine who would do such a thing.' But as she spoke a mental picture of Pat Daniels invaded her thoughts. But why would he do something like this? And she dismissed the notion.

The night porter let her in at the Langford Hotel when she rang the bell and then alerted her stepfather.

Luke came rushing down to the reception, hurriedly tying the belt of his dressing gown. 'Victoria! What's happened?'

She told him briefly.

'You looked exhausted,' he said. He asked the night porter for a key to a vacant room and told Victoria to go to bed. 'I'll see you in the morning.'

'I haven't a toothbrush,' she said and thought how stupid it sounded.

'There's one in every room, as for make-up, see your mother in the morning. She's asleep right now and I don't want to wake her. Tomorrow will be soon enough to tell her what's happened.' He took her to her room and kissed her on the cheek. 'Try and get some sleep, I'll see you when you wake.'

Victoria was now so tired that she took off her clothes and climbed straight into bed, too weary to think . . . and fell into a deep sleep.

In the morning, Lily knocked on Victoria's door and hurried in and sat on the bed.

'Luke told me what happened, how awful for you! Are you all right?'

Rubbing her eyes, Victoria sat up. 'Yes, just a bit shaken that's all. It's an awful feeling knowing that strangers have been through your things.' Frowning she said, 'I am so sorry but Luke's lovely mirrors were smashed to smithereens.'

Lily dismissed her worries. 'For goodness' sake, darling, that doesn't matter a fig! It's not important. Is anything missing?'

'I don't know yet, the detective wouldn't let me look until they'd been in and done their job.'

'Yes quite right. When they say you can go back to the flat, I'll come with you.'

'Will you?' Victoria looked relieved. She'd been dreading going into her flat alone. 'I'll ring George and tell him what happened and that I probably won't be in today, but I need a change of clothes and some make-up.'

'Come along to my room when you're ready, fortunately we are much the same size and you can use my stuff. I'll call the police station and ask when you can return if you like.'

Johnny Daniels met one of his clients in the Club Valletta where they planned to lunch and discuss business. It was the barman who told him what had happened.

'Mr Coleman was told this morning. Seems the flat's been well and truly trashed.'

'Is Miss Teglia all right?'

'Yes, sir. She's at her mother's place.'

Immediately after his business luncheon was over, Johnny drove to the Langford Hotel and spoke to the receptionist, who called Victoria's room. She asked for him to be sent up to her.

When she opened the door, Johnny took her into his arms. 'Are you all right, darling?'

Any animosity she may have felt towards him melted as he held her. 'I'm a bit shaken to be truthful. You'd better come in.' She proceeded to tell him what happened.

'But who would do such a thing? Do you keep anything of value there?' he asked.

Shaking her head she said, 'No, only clothes. Any spare money I keep in the safe in my office.' She hesitated. 'You don't think your father had anything to do with this, do you?'

'Dad?' He looked surprised. 'Why would he be mixed up in this?'

'I don't know. Call it a gut feeling if you like, but he was the first person I thought of. I'm sorry.'

At that moment Lily knocked on the door. When she saw Johnny she was taken aback. 'Good afternoon, Mr Daniels. This is a surprise.'

'I heard about the break in when I was at the club, I rushed over to see that Victoria was all right.'

'She's fine, thank you.' Turning to her daughter, she said, 'The police say you can now return to the flat so when you're ready we'll go.'

'Let me drive you both there,' Johnny quickly offered.

Lily was about to refuse but Victoria accepted before she could say anything, and the three of them drove there together. When they arrived and Victoria opened the door, both Lily and Johnny were shocked at the mayhem before their eyes. They looked at each other, then at Victoria who, having seen the mess for the second time, was furious.

'How dare they do this to me?' She stepped gingerly into the room being careful of the broken glass littering the carpet. 'This is wanton destruction!' she cried.

'Let's try and tidy the place up,' suggested Johnny. 'Then you will be able to see if there is anything missing.' And the three of them set to, to clear the debris.

Eventually, Victoria was able to search through her things. 'Nothing seems to have been taken,' she declared. 'All the drawers in my bedroom have been emptied, clothes tipped out, more things broken but, as far as I can see, that's it. There were one or two things in my jewellery box, but they were on the floor and broken, not taken. It doesn't make sense.'

Johnny was quiet. It didn't make any sense to him either. The broken mirrors were expensive. One or two porcelain figures would have earned a few pounds to a burglar, but they were just broken. It was almost as if Victoria was being sent a message . . . but what about?

'Where is the engagement ring that Bruce gave you?' Lily suddenly asked.

'Oh my God! I forgot about that,' said Victoria and she rushed to a small bureau in the corner where the top was open and papers strewn about. She opened a small drawer. 'It's gone! As far as I can tell, it's the only thing missing.'

'But no one would break in and take just one object when there are other pieces that would have brought in hard cash,' Lily said. She looked at Johnny Daniels. 'Don't you think that's strange?' There was a challenge in her expression as she waited for his reply.

He knew from her past experience with the underworld she thought the same as he did. 'Yes, I do find it strange.'

'What are you both trying to say?' Victoria demanded.

'This is like a warning,' said Johnny. 'But about what – and by whom?'

Her nostrils flared with anger. 'What about those two thugs who came to the club wanting me to pay for protection?'

'What two thugs? I never heard about this?' Lily looked at her daughter, demanding an answer.

Victoria explained what had happened and how Johnny had intervened.

Lily glared at him. 'Do you think this gang had anything to do with this?

He shook his head. 'No, I don't. I went round to see Max Reynolds and had a chat with him.'

'In other words, you threatened him.' Lily was defiant.

'If you like to put it that way . . . yes I did.' His gaze didn't flinch from hers.

'But who else would have a reason but him?' Victoria now intervened. 'No one else has caused me any trouble.'

'You must tell the police about this,' Lily insisted. Turning to Johnny she added, 'I'm sorry to involve you with this but you must see that is the only thing to do?'

How could he say differently? 'Yes, of course.' But he didn't like it. He would have preferred to have handled this himself. Now he would be called in to be questioned and that would put him in a bad light with the law, especially with his background. Up until now, he'd been able to put that behind him running a successful business, away from London and his father. Now, once again, he'd be under suspicion. He, above all, wanted to know who was behind this, who had placed him in this insidious position. Now it was he who was angry.

Seventeen

Once Victoria had reported the theft of her engagement ring and told the police about the visitation of the two men and Johnny Daniels' intervention, they asked him to come to the station and give a statement. He went along, albeit reluctantly. Detective Inspector Bill Cole, the man in charge of the case, took him into an interview room and asked him to sit down.

'Let's begin with the two men who came to the club, shall we?'

Johnny told him what happened and what he said to them to make them leave. There was no point at pretence, the police were well aware of his lineage.

'I believe your father was in Southampton recently,' Cole said. 'You met at the Club Valletta.'

'Yes, that's right. He wanted to discuss some business with me.'

The detective raised his eyebrows. 'Really? What kind of business?'

'We are both in construction and he was having problems with delivery dates, he wondered if I was in the same boat, that's all. If our deliveries don't arrive on time, it sends work schedules up the spout and makes for dissatisfied customers and neither of us want that.'

'We've made some enquiries about your business, Mr Daniels; you have a good reputation in the town it seems.'

'I hope so, my business depends on it.'

'Then why did you mention your father to these two men? This wouldn't help your reputation.'

'These men were thugs, they only understand one language.'

'As you would well know, being the son of one of London's major villains.'

Johnny looked at the detective and quietly said, 'My father has yet to be charged with any villainy – as far as I know.'

'Let's not beat about the bush, Daniels, we both know what your father is. Now, I want to know what you said when you went to see Max Reynolds.'

'I warned him about doing any harm to the Club Valletta.'

'In other words, you threatened him.'

'No, Inspector, I warned him. Miss Teglia and I are close; I was just looking after her interests, that's all.'

Bill Cole sat back in his chair with a bemused expression. 'Life's strange, don't you think? You, the son of a villain – she, the daughter of another.'

'Neither father ever charged with a misdemeanour, you should remember that, too. Besides, I run my own business and so does Miss Teglia; neither have anything to do with our fathers.'

'That would be difficult in her case, her old man died when she was a baby, but she still has his blood in her veins. But I digress. For now I need a statement from you as to what happened when you took Miss Teglia and her mother back to the flat and discovered the loss of her ring. I'll be visiting Mr Reynolds and will give him a warning. I'm not having trouble from him on my patch.' He stared at Johnny. 'You best think about that, too, Mr Daniels.'

'I'm in Southampton to do a good job for my clients, that's all. My business is a legitimate one. I would like *you* to remember *that!*'

'As long as it stays that way, I'll be a happy chappy. Now I'll get my man to give you a pad and pen.'

Johnny was left alone for a moment. He breathed a sigh of relief. Police stations made him nervous. He wrote out his statement on the pad he was given and left the building. Once outside, he lit a cigarette and walked quickly away. Damn, he thought. He'd hoped to have kept clear of any police involvement during his time here, but now they would be on his tail always. But he still had one problem. Who had trashed Victoria's flat and why? He would fix an alarm system for her and check on the one she had at the club too, because he felt that this was only the beginning. But when he arrived at the club, George Coleman was there. He strode over to Johnny.

'A word . . . in my office.'

George closed the door behind them. 'Do you know anything about this break in?'

'No of course I don't! Look, George, I love Victoria, I wouldn't harm a hair on her head, you've *got* to believe me.'

The older man saw the sincerity in his face and did believe him. 'So what the bloody hell is going on?'

'I don't know but the whole thing smells to me.' And he told him why. He also told him about Max Reynolds and the two men who called when George was away. 'I can't honestly believe it was them. Not after I saw Max.'

'So, who would have a motive to harm or cause Victoria trouble? She must be in somebody's way,' George remarked.

Johnny shook his head. 'Beats me. After all, she just runs the club; she doesn't step on anyone's toes, so who could have it in for her?'

George shook his head. 'I'll do some asking around.'

Sandy moved back to Southampton the next day and, once he'd unpacked his things, he walked along Bernard Street to see Victoria, but it was George Coleman he saw first and heard about the break in.

'This was no ordinary burglary,' George said. 'Stuff of value was just trashed . . . apart from Bruce's engagement ring which was taken. For the life of me I can't think of any motive.'

'Maybe I can,' said Sandy.

Coleman was immediately watchful. 'Then talk to me.'

'Old man Daniels isn't best pleased with his son at the moment, thinks he's getting too big for his boots.'

'I don't see the connection.' George looked puzzled.

'Pat knows he's sweet on Victoria. What better way of getting at Johnny, but through her?'

'Are you serious?'

Shrugging Sandy asked, 'Can you think of a better reason?'

'But Pat is big league; he wouldn't send his men to do such a menial task.'

'Maybe he got someone local to do it for him?' Sandy suggested.

'Like who?'

'I've no idea, to be honest.' Sandy pondered on the problem. 'Well I'll be doing the rounds tonight, let my mates know I'm back in circulation. Maybe I'll hear something. Give Victoria my love.'

Johnny, meantime, was up a ladder, fixing an alarm system at Victoria's flat. She watched with interest. This was another side to him she'd not seen and it intrigued her.

'I had no idea you were so proficient,' she remarked with some amusement.

He paused and stepped down from the ladder to pick up some wire. 'You seem to forget, darling, that I have to earn a living. I've been in this business since I was a young lad, helping my dad.'

At the mention of his father, Victoria's smile faded. 'Tell me about him.'

Climbing back up the ladder, Johnny said, 'Not much to tell really. He's a hard man to know. There wasn't a lot of affection in our house for me or my mother.'

'I thought he looked cruel,' she said quietly. 'He was polite. But although he smiled, his eyes were cold. I got the feeling he didn't like me.'

Johnny paused for just a second in his work, then carried on. 'Whatever do you mean?'

'I don't know, just a gut feeling, that's all.'

'I shouldn't worry about that. My father doesn't like many

people at all. He doesn't have the time or the inclination to try. His life is his business.'

Victoria would have liked to question him further about just what kind of business, but thought better of it. Since the break in she and Johnny had made up and she didn't want to spoil the closeness they had now.

A ring at the doorbell stopped any further conversation anyway. Johnny immediately got down from the ladder.

'I'll get that,' he said sharply.

'It's probably my taxi,' she called after him.

And so it was. She kissed him and said, 'I am going to work. Look in later if you can.'

When he was alone, he sat down and thought about her comments about Pat. He remembered the disparaging remarks his father had made about Victoria and frowned. Surely he wouldn't have been behind the break in? What reason would he have had? It was ridiculous. He climbed back up the ladder.

It was Saturday night and the club was packed. The tables were fully booked, as were the rooms. The three-piece band was playing and the gaming room was in full swing. Henry Charterhouse and Roger Bentley were there with some friends, playing roulette when George Coleman walked over to them.

'Ever get any news about the robbery, sir?' He asked Henry.

'No, George, the blighters got away with it. I wish I'd had the new alarm system that Roger and my friend in Romsey had fitted. My goodness, young Daniels was a great help.'

'Mr Daniels?'

'Yes, after my bad luck he suggested this new alarm just on the market. By Jove it seems to have worked because Edward Mansfield thinks someone was looking his property over at one time. A couple of chaps got talking to his chef in a bar and he let slip they had this system. It only came to light when his housekeeper refused entry to two men after he left instructions that no one was to be allowed in the house without his permission. We put two and two together.'

George Coleman walked slowly away, going over in his mind the information he'd been given, trying to make sense of it all.

Victoria was walking among the tables making sure her

clients were happy when she saw the door open and Bruce Chapman, dressed in civvies, walk in. Her heart seemed to miss a beat and her breath catch in her throat. It had been some time since she broke off her engagement and his appearance took her by surprise. She walked over to the bar where he was ordering a drink.

'Hello, Bruce, you're looking very smart. It's strange to see you out of uniform.'

He turned at the sound of her voice.

'Hello, Victoria.' He smiled fondly at her. 'How lovely you look, how are you?'

Gazing at the man who'd meant so much to her for so long, there was a strange feeling of comfort and familiarity. She *was* pleased to see him, which unnerved her a little.

'I'm fine, this is a surprise.'

'I've just got back to base after being away on manoeuvres and I longed to see you.' He reached out and took her hand. 'Have a drink with an old friend?'

'Of course, my usual.'

They found a vacant space and sat down.

'I'm happy to find you alone,' he quipped. 'I thought your new boyfriend might be in attendance.' He said this without animosity and she had to laugh.

'We don't spend every minute of the day together.'

'So he's still in the picture then?'

'Yes, I'm afraid so, Bruce.'

'Would that stop you from coming out with me tomorrow? Only I'm soon to be stationed in Malta for some time and it would be nice to see you at least once before I leave.'

Victoria didn't feel she could refuse and in any case she wanted to catch up on his news. Bruce would always be a part of her life although they were no longer engaged.

'That would be lovely, what had you in mind?'

'How about a trip to Lymington? I can get hold of an admiralty car; it seems a pity not to take advantage of that. I could pick you up about ten o'clock at your place.'

'I'll look forward to it. Look, I'm sorry but I have to get back to work, as you can see we have a full house tonight.'

'No, that's fine; we'll talk some more tomorrow.'

He watched her walk away knowing he was still in love with her.

Promptly at ten o'clock the next morning, Bruce was at Victoria's flat as planned and they drove through the New Forest to Lymington, parked the car and walked around the small town, stopping for coffee at a small cafe near the harbour.

It was a bright day and the sun shone over the yachts tied up at the jetties. A soft breeze caressed the halyards and rustled among the sails. It was a peaceful and picturesque scene to gaze at as they sat together chatting.

Bruce was telling Victoria about his days spent at sea on manoeuvres . . . and how he'd missed her. 'To be honest, Victoria, when you broke our engagement, I was glad to get away, only you came with me. Like it or not, you are part of me and I missed you more than I can say.'

She felt dreadful. 'I am so sorry, Bruce. When I accepted your proposal, I didn't envisage anything other than spending my life with you, but . . .' She didn't know what else to say.

'Then Johnny Daniels came along!'

She just nodded.

'So what else has happened in your life since last we met?' he asked, not wanting to talk further about the man who came between them.

She told him about the break in of her flat.

He was appalled. 'Thank God you weren't there! What are the police doing about it?'

She explained. 'But Mother and Johnny think the whole thing very odd.' And she told him why.

'A warning?' His brow furrowed with concern. 'Has anything else happened since?'

She shook her head. 'No, everything has been quiet on that front.'

'Do you think it has anything to do with Daniels?'

'Johnny? Why would it?'

'Well, darling, he is connected to that kind of world after all. This worries me, Victoria.'

She was immediately defensive. 'Only through his father! He has a legitimate business and is as concerned as I am.'

Bruce wasn't convinced. 'Are the police giving you any protection?'

'For goodness' sake, it was only a break in, stop being so bloody dramatic! George is always at the club and . . .'

'Johnny is with you outside, I suppose?'

'Not all the time, he does have a business to run and anyway it's not necessary. I've not personally been threatened, you know.'

He laughed. 'Sorry. I can't help it, I still feel responsible for you. Come on, let's go for a walk round the harbour, then later we'll have lunch somewhere.' And he dropped the subject.

It was an enjoyable day; both of them so used to one another, and as the day progressed it was as if they'd never been apart. They laughed together, teased one another, enjoyed walking around together and when Bruce took her hand it was such a natural thing to do, Victoria didn't even notice. They stopped in a small pub in Brockenhurst for a drink before driving home.

'Come in for a coffee before you go back to Portsmouth.' Victoria suggested.

Once inside the flat, Bruce was aware of the things that were missing and was again worried. But he kept his thoughts to himself.

They sat on the sofa together, drank their coffee and talked about their day.

'It was like old times,' he said softly and, putting his arm around her, kissed her gently. 'Wherever I am, Victoria, if ever you need me all you have to do is pick up the phone. I'll give you a number to call when I go to Malta.'

She gazed fondly at him. 'You would do that for me, even after everything?'

'Yes, darling, and if things get difficult, you could always come out to me, you know.' Seeing her worried frown he added, 'I had hoped you would come with me as my wife, but if you need a bolt hole for any reason, I want you to promise me you'll get in touch.'

She was overcome at his generosity under the circumstances. 'I don't know what to say, Bruce.'

'Just promise that you will, that's all.'

'I promise.'

'I will try and see you again before I go, if that's all right?'

'Don't you dare leave without saying goodbye,' she retorted.

At the front door, he took her into his arms and kissed her longingly. 'Do make sure you're not making a big mistake, darling.'

Before she could answer, the doorbell rang. Seeing the look of alarm that flashed in her eyes, Bruce said, 'I'll answer that.'

He opened the door. 'Hello, Daniels,' he said.

Eighteen

Johnny looked flabbergasted as he saw who had opened Victoria's flat door. 'What the devil are *you* doing here?' he demanded.

'Just leaving old man,' said Bruce with a grin. Turning to Victoria he said, 'Thank you for a lovely day, see you soon.'

Johnny strode into the flat. 'What the hell is going on?'

Victoria started laughing. 'You should see the look on your face!'

'What's so bloody funny?'

'Well, Johnny, it reminded me of the time Bruce and I were having dinner in the Cowherds before we broke up and you deliberately came over and mentioned we'd been out together. Now Bruce has turned the tables by doing exactly the same to you, the only difference was – he didn't blow a gasket!' She walked back into the lounge, still chuckling.

'So where *have* you been?'

'To the New Forest and Lymington. We had a lovely day, thanks for asking.'

He grabbed her roughly by her wrist. 'Don't play games with me, Victoria. What were you doing spending the day with him?'

'Let go of me!'

'Not until you tell me what's going on!'

Seeing the anger flashing in his eyes, she answered. 'Nothing is *going* on as you seem to be suggesting. I went out with an old friend that's all, now let *go* of me.'

He did so and she rubbed her sore wrist, which was reddened by the force with which he'd held her. Now she was the one who was angry. 'Don't you dare use strong-arm tactics with me, Johnny, because I certainly won't tolerate them.'

'Sorry, but I was shocked to see him here in your flat. I thought it was over between you two. Now I don't know what to think.'

She tried to explain. 'Bruce is being posted to Malta very soon, he just wanted to say goodbye. There was nothing more to it than that. You forget, Johnny, Bruce and I were together for a long time before I met you.'

'Oh, believe me, I haven't forgotten. You may think you've broken up with him, but does he?'

Victoria remembered her conversation with Bruce and didn't reply. Despite everything, he'd offered her a sanctuary should she need it and deep down she knew that was more than just friendship.

'You are being ridiculous!' she exclaimed.

Johnny reached out and this time his touch was gentle. 'I'm sorry, but seeing you together . . . I love you, Victoria, I don't want to lose you.'

She capitulated. 'Now you really are being ridiculous. What are you doing here, anyway?'

'They told me at the club you had taken the day off; I wondered if you were all right, so I came to find out. Thankfully you are.' He released her and walked away. 'Sorry, I'm just a bit edgy after the break in.'

'Oh, that's really sweet of you, but please stop worrying about me, nothing's going to happen, whatever you think it was just a burglary and nothing more.'

But when the following morning she arrived at the club to find that someone had managed to get to the cellar by way of the loading bay for the barrels of beer and had removed the stoppers to some of the kegs, nearly flooding the place, Victoria *did* begin to worry.

★   ★   ★

Sandy had been doing the rounds of his old haunts, getting back into the swing of things, catching up with old friends, asking questions and finding one or two interesting answers.

Max Reynolds, it appeared, was causing a minor stir, swanning around the place, full of himself. Hinting that he had the backing of someone important, yet not giving anything more away. The members of the Southampton underworld were getting heartily sick of this newcomer among their midst and Sandy sensed a feeling of growing menace among this undesirable crowd and he didn't like it. He said as much to George Coleman the next day when he went to report his findings. It was then he heard about the destruction of the beer barrels.

'This is all small stuff,' said George. 'You know how it goes, little things meant to unsettle you, wondering what's going to happen next. But what worries me, Sandy, is just what *is* going to happen next. I think I'll go along and see this Reynolds.'

'Do the police know what's happened?'

'Of course, I reported it straight away.'

'Then, my friend, your intervention may be unwise. Just think, George, you have a business to run, don't jeopardize that position. This isn't the old days, you know.'

Coleman gave a sly grin. 'There's more than one way to skin a cat, Sandy.'

That evening, Reynolds walked back to his home alone. He'd decided to have a quiet night and keep a low profile for a few days. He put the key into the lock and opened his front door when suddenly he was pushed into the hall and held up against the wall. He'd not had time to switch the hall light on, but from the low light from the street lamp outside he could see enough to recognize George Coleman. Coleman's reputation was enough to chill his blood.

'What do you want?' he asked nervously.

'You and me are going to have a little chat,' said George, and he pinned the man's arms behind and shoved him into the back room. Pulling out a chair, he pushed Reynolds into it.

'Now what's your game?'

'Don't know what you mean,' spluttered Max.

George held him by the throat and began to squeeze. 'Don't be stupid, lad. Let's try again, shall we?'

Reynolds could feel the leather of the glove tighten and he fought for breath. 'I can't breathe,' he cried.

'Unless you start talking, you won't ever breathe again,' said George and slightly released his hold. 'Who's behind your little game and don't pretend you don't know what I'm talking about.' And he tightened his hold.

'All right, all right! Reynolds was scared out of his wits.

'Talk to me!' Coleman demanded.

'He'll kill me if I talk,' he protested.

'And I'll kill you if you don't. Your choice.' Coleman squeezed a bit harder.

That was enough to loosen the thug's tongue. 'It was Pat Daniels. He asked me to put the frighteners on the girl from the club.'

This took George by surprise. 'Why?'

'He wanted to teach his son a lesson. Seems young Johnny wants to go straight instead of being the eyes for his father here and at the club among the toffs.'

Suddenly it all made sense to George and he let the man go.

Reynolds fell forward gasping for breath. 'You bastard Coleman, you nearly did for me!'

'That was my intention,' he answered coldly. 'What did he promise you in return?'

'He said he'd take care of me.'

'I bet he did and you thought he meant that in a nice way.'

'What do you mean?' Reynolds looked terrified.

'You surely didn't think he'd keep you around after you'd done his dirty work? He wouldn't want any loose ends my friend. You are disposable . . . didn't you realize that?'

Max remembered Daniels saying that no way was anything to tie him in with the job in hand and he cursed. 'What should I do?'

'Get out of Southampton as far away as you can and lie low. That's if you want to reach old age.' He turned and left.

As he walked back to the club through the darkened docklands, George was trying to think of how to deal with this information. Nothing would be achieved by his facing the London mobster, he no longer had a strong-arm team behind him and anyway, he needed to keep his nose clean. If he got too involved the future of the Club Valletta would be in jeopardy and he needed to maintain a clean record. But he also needed to protect Victoria. There was only one person who could deal with this head on.

Johnny Daniels was surprised to receive a call from George Coleman and even more so when he asked Johnny to meet him in The Lord Roberts in Canal Walk. But it was nothing to the shock he had when, seated together, Coleman told him what he'd learned.

'My father? He's behind all this. Are you sure?'

'Makes perfect sense to me, son. Let's be honest, you set up the robbery at Henry Charterhouse's place, I knew that deep in my bones . . . now don't deny it!'

Johnny met the older man's gaze. There was no point in a denial – not now. 'Yes, I did, and I deeply regret that, but I tried to stop the other two.'

'Yes, I heard about the new alarm system, that must have pissed off your old man.'

Johnny smiled ruefully. 'Yes, in no uncertain terms. That's when I told the old man I wanted out because of Victoria.'

George sat back with a look of satisfaction. 'There you go then, that explains it all. So what are you going to do about it? No one else is better placed to sort this.'

Inwardly, Johnny was seething to think his father could have pulled such a stroke.

'What about Max Reynolds?'

George laughed heartily. 'He's so scared I thought he'd mess his pants. He's just a bag of hot air, by now he'll be long gone. Just as well because he was getting up the noses of a few undesirables and it would have become messy. It's just your dad you have to deal with . . . are you man enough?'

'Oh yes. You see, George, I know too much. I know where all the bodies are buried – figuratively speaking. I could put my father behind bars if I had a mind to!'

Leaning forward George issued a warning. 'You be very

careful, lad. Your old man is a tough nut; he won't take kindly to any threats.'

Johnny knew this was sound advice. He would have to tread very carefully. He thought for a moment, then suddenly grinned. 'As you are always saying, George, there's more than one way to skin a cat!'

Pat Daniels was in his warehouse with a couple of his men, collecting materials for his next job, when, to his surprise, a couple of police cars pulled up and a detective came over to him.

'Mr Patrick Daniels?'

'Yes, that's right, who wants to know?'

The detective handed him a paper. 'I have a warrant to search your premises.'

'You what?'

The detective ignored him and beckoned the team of waiting constables into the building. 'Be very thorough,' he told them. I don't want you to miss anything.'

Pat watched in horror as the men systematically started their search. One of the two men with him began to say something but Pat shut him up, lit a cigarette, and watched carefully.

The building was huge, with building materials stacked high. There were stacks of building bricks, bags of cement, iron girders, casement windows and all manner of tools a construction business of this magnitude might need.

The following hours passed slowly, the searchers getting tired, the detective getting edgy when nothing untoward was to be found. Pat Daniels just watched, silently. His office had been inspected inch by inch, but there was nothing incriminating there.

One of the constables approached the detective and quietly said, 'The place is clean, sir, as far as we can see.'

The detective looked grim but determined. 'We haven't finished yet. Carry on.'

Half an hour later there was a cry from the far corner of the warehouse.

'Sir, over here.'

Pat Daniels looked over and stiffened as the constable pulled out a small wooden crate and forced it open. They all watched in silence as he produced two books.

The detective studied it and smiled to himself. He carried it over to Daniels. 'If my information is correct, these belong to Henry Charterhouse. They were stolen along with a small Goya painting.'

Daniels feigned surprise. 'I've never seen these before in my life,' he insisted.

'No, of course you haven't. I need you to accompany me to the station for further questioning.'

'Am I under arrest?' Daniels asked.

'Not yet,' said the detective. 'Are you going to give me any trouble?'

'Why should I? I've nothing to hide.' Daniels smirked, but his eyes remained cold.

It wasn't long before news filtered through to Johnny that his father had been taken to a London police station. One of Pat's men rang Johnny's office to tell him.

'Questioning about what?' he asked.

The man didn't want to discuss it over the telephone, so Johnny just asked him to let him know what happened. He placed the receiver on its cradle and smiled. And when, later that evening, he told George Coleman what had happened – he, too, smiled.

'Nice work, son,' he said and walked away.

Nineteen

Pat Daniels was being interrogated thoroughly by the detective and his colleague, but he continued to deny any knowledge of the two stolen first editions.

'How long are you going to keep up this ridiculous pretence?' asked the detective. 'There is no way the books could have been stashed in your warehouse without your knowledge. You're just wasting my time.'

But Daniels would not be moved and challenged the detective. 'Prove it!'

The detective looked at him with some disdain. 'Not necessary. I'm charging you with possession of stolen goods. Read him his rights,' he told the man beside him, 'then take him to a cell. I've had enough of him.'

'I want my solicitor,' Daniels declared.

The detective got to his feet. 'You certainly will need him. When you've finished here,' he told his man, 'let him make the call.'

After Daniels had made his call and was led away to a cell, he inwardly fumed. Someone must have given the police information or why would they have suddenly arrived, mob handed, at the warehouse? But who? It had to be an insider. No one else knew. None of his men would have squealed to the coppers, he'd stake his life on that, which only left one person. His son. His eyes narrowed. Would Johnny have dropped him in it? Only if he'd discovered that he was behind the burglary of the Teglia girl's flat and the flooding of the beer cellar. If this was the case, was he so smitten with his girl that he'd put his own father behind bars?

Johnny received a call from his father's solicitor later that day. He sat in his office and listened.

'Your father is being charged with being in possession of stolen property,' he was told.

'Oh, and what was the property?' Johnny asked, knowing the answer.

The solicitor told him.

'What are his chances?' he asked.

'He has no chance, if you want my opinion. The police have been after him for some time, they won't let this charge go away.'

'Well, I suppose he'll just have to suck his teeth and do the time.'

He heard the surprise in the other man's voice. 'Well I must say your lack of concern is surprising; he is your father after all.'

Years of pent up frustration surfaced. 'He's never been a real father to me,' Johnny declared. 'He has never shown an atom of love for either me or my mother. He's a hard man and you know it. He's been bloody lucky for a very long time and now it's run out!'

'He wants to see you.'

Johnny sat back and considered this request, then he spoke. 'I can't get away at the moment, I'm too busy. I'll try and make it to the courthouse when his case comes up, if you let me know when.' He replaced the receiver.

His father would never forgive him, he knew that, but he had no love for Pat. He'd never been able to please him even as a child when he'd striven for his father's approval and now it was payback. Pat chose his way of life, had dragged his son into the business and now he would have to pay the price for a life of crime. Johnny thought his father had got off lightly. If the police knew all about his father's past crimes, he would go down for years. Well, he'd be a good son and never tell . . . unless he was really pushed. Only one thing worried him: he'd have to come clean with Victoria and tell him about his father's incarceration. He would have to confess to being involved with the burglary at Henry Charterhouse's residence. How would she take it? There was only one way to find out.

Later that evening, Johnny made his way to the Club Valletta with some trepidation. His whole future depended on tonight. He'd put his father behind bars for Victoria; would she appreciate what he had done for her? He walked slowly towards her office.

Victoria looked up as there was a tap on her door and Johnny stepped inside. She looked happy to see him and he wondered how long that would last.

'Have you got a minute?' he asked.

He looked so serious she wondered what was wrong. 'Of course, close the door and sit down.'

He walked round the desk, perched on the end of it and took her hand in his.

'Whatever is the matter?' she asked.

'Before I tell you, I want you to know that I love you very much and I would die rather than have anyone hurt you.'

Her heart sank. Whatever was he going to tell her?

'When I first came to the club, I was working for my father. Some of your clientele are wealthy men and I was to find those who had money and property which held things of value, stuff that would sell to customers who wouldn't ask any questions.'

Victoria started to speak but he hushed her. 'Please, darling, listen to what I have to say, then you can talk,' he asked. 'I'm afraid I was the cause of the burglary at Henry Charterhouse's home. I passed information on to my father, about his wealth and . . . well, you know the rest.' He gazed at her and hurried on. 'But then I realized that I had deep feelings for you and I went to my father and asked him not to continue with his plans.'

'What plans?' asked Victoria as she withdrew her hand from his.

'I had given him two more addresses. But I didn't trust him so I made sure these men installed a brand new alarm system that my father's men wouldn't be able to break.'

Victoria looked at him coldly. 'Go on.'

'Well, then your flat was trashed.'

She looked at him, understanding beginning to dawn on her.

'As you now know, I discovered who had done this and went to call on him, as I told the police. But later, after the beer barrels had been tampered with, it was discovered he was working for my father.'

'What?' She looked horrified.

'He was trying to get to me through you. Well, Victoria, I couldn't possibly have that!'

'So what did you do, Johnny?' The icy tone in her voice chilled him to the bone. I've lost her, he thought – but he carried on.

'I made an anonymous call to the police and told them where the stolen first editions were being kept – in my father's warehouse. They got a warrant and searched it. They found them and, at this moment, my father is sitting in a cell in a London prison, waiting to be sent to trial for being in possession of stolen goods.'

Victoria was finding it difficult to take all this in. 'You shopped your own father?'

'I had to! He wouldn't listen to me, he didn't want me to leave his organization and make an honest living. That he couldn't understand – and he certainly didn't want me to be involved with you. He's a very possessive man.'

He saw the look of consternation in her eyes.

'I do love you, Victoria. I couldn't let him put you in danger, I couldn't!'

She didn't know what to say.

'Look, I know this has come as a shock to you, but I have been honest. I have cut myself off from my father because I love you and now I want different things from life. I hope you can understand what I'm trying to say. When you've had time to digest all this, call me . . . and please – don't break my heart.' He leaned forward and kissed her forehead, than left the office.

George Coleman saw him walk out of the club, noted the unusual slump of his shoulders and knew that something was amiss. He walked to the office and entered.

He looked at Victoria and asked, 'What's wrong?'

She gazed up at the man she'd known from a child, a man she trusted with her life – and told him.

George listened carefully until she'd finished. 'So how do you feel about all this?' he asked.

'I wish I knew,' she confessed. Then, shaking her head, she added, 'How could I ever trust him again?'

He stared hard at her. 'Don't you realize just what this lad has done because he loves you?'

'What do you mean?'

'Listen, when he first came here I didn't either trust or like him, if I'm honest. In fact, I went out of my way to let him know this, but I have to tell you, Victoria, I now admire him and I *do* trust him. Pat Daniels is not a man to cross. His men are scared witless of him. He has a fearful reputation, and Johnny has not only broken with him but put the bugger behind bars! He has put himself in danger over you, do you realize that?'

'What do you mean, in danger?'

'Pat Daniels won't let him get away with this. It's not in his nature.'

'Oh my God! What will he do?'

Shrugging, George said, 'To be honest I don't know, but if I was young Daniels I'd be looking over my shoulder a lot and wouldn't walk down any dark alleyways, that's for sure.'

'But his father is going to prison. I don't know for how long but he'll be out of the way. Johnny will be safe for a while.'

George looked at her with affection. 'You have no idea, have you? Many a job has been run by a gangster who was inside. If old man Daniels has a mind to do something, being inside will make no difference, he'll just give the orders.'

'So what can we do?' She suddenly had an idea. 'What if Johnny was out of the country for a while?'

'What are you driving at?'

'Bruce is being stationed in Malta; he told me that if I ever needed a bolt hole I could go to him.'

George looked at her in disbelief. 'You would ask Bruce to help the man who broke up his engagement? I can't believe you would be so heartless . . . anyway, I doubt if Johnny would go. He's made of stern stuff; to run away wouldn't be his style.' He looked hard at her. 'I wonder if you know this lad at all, if you could believe that.'

And he left her alone feeling like a child who had been scolded. But he had made his point and Victoria began to understand just how serious a step Johnny had taken – because of her.

'He said what?' Pat Daniels looked at his solicitor as they sat in an interview room in Wandsworth prison.

'He said he was too busy to get away at the moment but he'd be in court when your case came up.' He thought his client was going to have a fit; his anger was such that his face was beetroot red and he seemed unable to breathe for a moment.

'That little bastard! Who the bloody hell does he think he is? How dare he treat me this way – his own father?'

'I'm sorry, Mr Daniels. I did as you asked me.'

But Daniels was still fuming. 'Well, I won't put up with it. The boy needs a lesson on who is boss and I'll see he gets one!'

'Now, please, don't consider doing anything foolish.' The solicitor was worried, knowing the man who sat before him. 'You don't want anything more for the police to be able to hold against you.'

Big Pat looked at him disdainfully. 'Don't be a bloody idiot! I know what I'm about. The only reason I'm in here is because of my son. Until now, the police have never been able to prove anything against me.'

'You don't know for certain that Johnny put you here.' The man was trying to diffuse the situation.

'Oh yes I do. None of my men would go against me. It's all because of a bit of pussy! My God, a woman would never come between *me* and my job.' He sat running his fingers through his hair in frustration.

The solicitor rose from his seat, gathered his papers together and started to walk towards the door. 'It'll be a few weeks before your case comes before the court. I'll be in to see you again before then.'

'They're going to send me down, aren't they?' the criminal asked.

'I'm afraid so. I'll do my best but I don't hold out much hope to be honest.'

The warder stepped forward and placed the handcuffs back on Daniels' wrists. Pat looked at the manacles and his features tightened in anger, but he didn't say a word as he was led away.

That evening, Johnny Daniels was sitting dejectedly in his flat, drinking a glass of whiskey when his front-door bell rang. Muttering under his breath, he went to the door and opened it.

'Hello, Johnny,' said Victoria, 'can I come in?'

'Are you sure you want to?' he asked.

'Excuse me?' She looked at him with raised eyebrows. 'What happened to the Daniels charm, I'd like to know? The Johnny I once knew would welcome me with bright eyes and high expectations, wondering how long it would take to get me into bed!'

A slow smile crept across his features as he stared at her. 'That's very true.' He held out his hand. 'How about thirty seconds?'

Twenty

Two days later Victoria received a call from Bruce Chapman. He was soon to leave for his posting in Malta and wanted to see her to say goodbye. They decided to meet in the cocktail bar of the Polygon Hotel. As she replaced the receiver, she remembered how she was going to use their relationship and ask him to supply a refuge for her lover and was full of remorse to think she could have been so tactless. She had treated Bruce so badly; the least she could do was send him off to Malta with good grace. Picking up her handbag she left the club.

When Victoria arrived at the Polygon, she saw Bruce sitting at the bar in conversation with the barman. Bruce was wearing his uniform and she couldn't help but think any woman would be proud to be on the arm of such a good-looking man. But she had turned him down. Nevertheless, he would always be very special to her, no matter what.

Touching him lightly on the shoulder she asked, 'Buy a lady a drink, Captain?'

He was delighted to see her and, leaning forward, he kissed her cheek. 'Any time, tiger, what'll it be?'

They settled at a table by the window.

He gazed admiringly at her. 'You look wonderful as always, darling. How are things?'

'Fine, thanks. Now tell me about your posting.'

'I'm likely to be in Malta for quite a while,' he said. 'Perhaps you'll be able to get away and visit me some time . . . a sort of holiday in the sun?'

Bruce had never been able to hide his feelings and she saw the longing in his eyes and was saddened. 'We'll see,' she said with some hesitation.

He tried to cover his feelings. 'What's up, tiger? Afraid you won't be able to resist me?' And he laughed.

She chuckled with some relief. 'You are so bad!'

He kept the conversation light. 'Well, you know, sex doesn't always have to have any strings attached. We could just have fun, enjoy each other as we have always done, then you could come home again having had a good time with an old friend.'

But behind his jollity, Victoria, who understood him so well, knew that he was still hurting and wished there was something she could do to change this, but it was too late.

'We'll always be friends, Bruce. Nothing will ever change that and one day you'll meet a good woman, one who is really worthy of you.'

All pretence fell away from the captain. 'I have already met that woman, Victoria. There will never be another who could ever mean so much to me.' He leaned forward so no one could hear him. 'It's not too late you know. We could still make a future together if you had a mind to.'

She was overcome with emotion and fought to keep it under control. 'I'm sorry, Bruce,' was all she could say.

He sat back, sipped his drink and smiled softly at her. Cocking his head to one side, he said, 'Well, it was worth a try. Come on, I've booked a table for lunch.' And he led her into the dining room.

Despite the continuing food rationing, the menu was not too bad. They joked about the rabbit on offer, wondering if the staff had been out shooting, then ordered the fish. Bruce chose a bottle of wine and they sat chatting about different things, carefully avoiding anything personal. As usual he made her laugh and they enjoyed the meal. Just as they had finished their dessert and were drinking coffee with a liqueur, Victoria saw a pageboy enter the dining room in his smart green uniform and pillbox hat. He was carrying a gift-wrapped parcel and a bouquet of flowers. She was astonished when he made his way to their table and presented her with these.

'For me? Are you sure?'

'Yes, madam,' was the reply and the boy walked away with a jaunty air. She looked at Bruce who was smiling at her bewilderment.

'Just something to remember me by,' he said.

She placed the flowers on an empty seat next to her and, still holding the large, flat box with its extravagant bow, felt just like a child at Christmas.

'Can I open it?' she asked breathlessly.

Bruce started laughing. 'You know you'll never be able to wait, carry on.'

She removed the bow and lifted the lid and started to remove the tissue paper.

Beneath the layer was an exquisite nightdress in the softest pale silver satin. She closed the lid quickly, her cheeks red with embarrassment and looked up at her companion.

'I bought it for you when we were in France but you had left for England before I could give it to you. I waited for the right moment – but now, I've run out of time.'

'Oh, Bruce, it's beautiful, thank you so much.'

'Well, darling, whenever you wear it, think of me.' He beckoned the head waiter over and asked for the bill. Then he ordered a taxi to take Victoria back to the club.

'I have an appointment,' he told her when they were outside, 'so I can't take you back myself.'

As the taxi drew up, he took her into his arms and kissed her longingly. 'You take good care of yourself and remember, I'll send you my address. If you need me, pick up the phone. Promise?'

She felt her eyes fill with tears. 'Yes, I promise. Now you take care, Bruce, and keep in touch.' Then quickly turning away, she climbed into the car.

As she was driven back to the docks, she wiped away the tears which slowly trickled down her cheeks. If only things were different, Bruce would have been such a great husband, but she had made her choice and she wondered just why life had to be so bloody difficult.

The next few weeks passed without incident and life carried on. Johnny's business was growing and he took on more men to cope with the extra work, Victoria worked hard in the club, trying to keep her clients happy with the odd themed evening to make things interesting and the cash flow healthy. There was a circus theme with the waiters dressed as clowns, a cabaret of tumblers, George was dressed as a ringmaster and a trapeze was set up on the stage with a female acrobat twisting and turning as the three-piece band played. It all added to the fun and her clients appreciated it. Life was difficult enough these days with all the restrictions still in place despite the ending of hostilities.

Victoria had invested some of her money in a smallholding which, run by a couple of ex-servicemen, supplied her restaurant with eggs from the chickens, some of which were bred for slaughter. Fortunately her chef was talented and as she often said 'could make a meal out of the contents of a dustbin!' All of which was appreciated by her clients. Especially the night the chef roasted a suckling pig, raised on the small holding. On that night the restaurant was fully booked!

Eventually Pat Daniels' case was due to be heard in court and his solicitor informed Johnny of the time and place. When he told Victoria about it, she offered to go with him.

He gave a wry smile. 'No, darling, that would not be a good idea. There is already enough bad feeling between my father and me. If he saw you sitting with me in court, it would be like a red rag to a bull!'

'Just you be careful,' she warned, her brow creased with concern.

He held her close. 'Don't you worry about me, Victoria; I can take care of myself.'

But when she mentioned this to George and Sandy, who had called into the club, George said, 'I'll go if you like, love.'

'I'll come with you,' said Sandy.

The spectator's gallery was full on the first day of Daniels' trial and the two men sat in the only empty seats left. They both leaned forward as Pat Daniels was led up the steps to the dock.

He was smartly dressed in a suit and tie. His polished shoes shone as a shaft of sunlight caught them, but his face was grim. He cast a gaze around the courtroom and stopped when he saw Johnny sitting there. He looked coldly at him and the two men sitting above glanced at each other.

'No love lost there then,' George remarked to Sandy, who just nodded in agreement.

The case only took three days before the jury were sent out for their deliberations. It didn't take many hours before they returned with a verdict of guilty. Pat Daniels stood as the judge prepared to sentence him. The prisoner didn't listen to the judge's summing up. He knew he was going down, all he wanted to know was for how long and when he heard the words 'three years', he stared over at Johnny and continued to look at him with an expression of hatred as he was led away.

'Oh my God!' muttered George Coleman. 'That lad is in serious trouble. Come on, let's get out of here and get a beer.'

As they stepped outside the court, they saw Johnny about to walk away and called him over.

'What on earth are you two doing here?' he asked.

'Victoria was worried about you, so we said we'd come along. We're going for a drink,' said George, 'come with us, after that I think you need one.' They walked away together to the nearest pub.

Once they were settled, George didn't waste any time in getting to the point.

'Your old man's got it in for you, son,' he said. 'What steps have you taken to protect yourself?'

Johnny didn't argue – he knew the score. His father would pay him back in spades for what he saw as a betrayal. 'At the moment, none,' he admitted.

'Then now is the time to do so,' George insisted. 'You know your old man; he won't let this pass, it's not in his nature. How far do you think he'll go?'

'Surely he wouldn't top his own son?' Sandy was aghast at such a thought.

George looked at Johnny. 'Would he?'

Johnny frowned and peered into the contents of his glass before he looked at Coleman. 'To be honest I wouldn't put anything past him. You saw the look he gave me.'

'Oh shit!' said Sandy.

'Right then.' George Coleman took charge. 'I have a few favours I can call in. You need someone at your back twenty-four hours of the day.'

Johnny looked astonished. 'You'd do that for me?'

Coleman laughed heartily. 'Strange, isn't it, considering the hard time I gave you when you first arrived on the scene?'

'You hated me!' Johnny declared.

'I did! But eventually you stopped being an arsehole and became a man! Besides, I have also to protect Victoria. She's involved with you and I don't want her near you if your dad sends someone to teach you a lesson, do I?'

Frowning, Johnny said, 'Perhaps it's best we don't see one another for a time.'

Sandy let out a snort of derision. 'Of course, you can see her agreeing to that . . . I don't think. Our girl has too much spirit for her own good!'

Johnny looked at George. 'If anything happened to her through me, I couldn't live with myself. What are we going to do?'

'Leave it to me, lad. I'll arrange for you to have a bodyguard with you at all times. There'll be a team of men lined up to do so. Just give me twenty-four hours. Your dad won't have time to do anything until he's been settled in his cell, that'll give me a bit of breathing space.'

'I don't know what to say, George.'

'Nothing to say, but you let my girl down – I'll top you myself!'

Sandy looked at the old-time gangster and knew he meant every word.

Once they returned to Southampton, George and Sandy told Victoria what had transpired. She listened carefully as they set out George's plan before her.

'It's really that serious do you think?'

'You should have seen the look old man Daniels gave his son,' said Sandy. 'He's an evil devil.'

'I'm not surprised,' Victoria told them. 'When I met him here, I thought he looked a cruel and dangerous man. Seems I was right. How long will you have to protect Johnny do you think?'

'Hard to say.' George admitted. 'A lot depends on whether Daniels can keep his boys together during his time inside.'

'What do you mean?' asked Victoria.

'Well, when the boss of a gang is sent down, sometimes the men get restless and, if they're any good, they get filtered into other organizations until, eventually, by the time the boss gets released, they've all gone. We'll have to wait and see.' He stroked his chin. 'I might be able to drop a word here and there to move that along.'

'Don't you start going back to your old ways, George.' Victoria warned him. 'You've been out of that way of life ever since my father died. Please don't do it,' she pleaded. 'I don't want you to get involved like that and neither would Johnny.'

He smiled benignly. 'Have no fear, love. It would be nothing more than a phone call to the right people, that's all.'

And with that, she had to be content, but later, when Victoria was alone, she worried about what lay ahead. How would Johnny's father get his revenge? She remembered the steely look in the man's eyes when last he'd spoken to her – and her blood chilled.

Lily Langford, Victoria's mother, read about Pat Daniels' case in the national newspaper. It made headlines and, as she read the account of the trial, she frowned. This was far too close to home and she was worried. She passed the paper to Luke who read it and then looked at her.

'Why are you looking so concerned?'

'To be honest, I don't really know, but I have a gut feeling about this and that makes me nervous.'

'Then give George Coleman a call, he'll be able to tell you if you have any reason to fret. Go on, do it now or you'll be like a scolded cat all day long and that's not good for my nerves!'

Lily went to her office and picked up the receiver.

It was Coleman who answered the phone. He listened to Lily and then told her what had transpired and the steps he'd taken to ensure Johnny Daniels' safe-keeping.

'I damn well knew this wasn't straight forward!' she exclaimed. 'Do you think my Victoria is in any danger?'

'Not directly,' he assured her, 'but of course if she's with the lad, that's a different kettle of fish, but . . . there'll be someone with them all the time.'

'Not if she stays overnight with him.'

'My man will be in either flat, Lily. Trust me, I've left no stone unturned. Relax. She'll be fine.'

But as she put down the receiver, Lily couldn't help but

worry. She understood the criminal world and the lengths that some would go to pay back any slight and Johnny had pulled the unforgivable sin, by shopping his own father. This was seriously bad news.

Twenty-One

Pat Daniels sat in the back of the Black Maria as it was driven away from the courthouse. Newspaper reporters held their cameras high towards the windows, trying to grab a picture of the well-known criminal inside. Daniels swore under his breath at the flashes from the cameras reflected against the darkened windows. His bloody son was going to pay for this!

His temper didn't abate as he was led into Wandsworth prison and made to empty his pockets. 'Sign here,' said the officer on duty who went through everything in detail. Then he was stripped of his clothes and made to take a shower before being bodily searched – which infuriated him. He snarled at the warders as they went about their business.

'You need to calm down, Daniels,' said one. 'In here, you're just a number, like all the others.'

'I am *not* like all the others!' he snapped.

'Suit yourself!' said his jailer. 'You'll soon learn.'

After being given a set of prison clothes, a pair of pyjamas and a change of underwear, plus a sheet and a couple of blankets, he was taken to a cell. As he walked along the alleyways, he caused quite a stir among the other inmates. They were heard to whisper among themselves. 'That's Pat Daniels! Never thought I'd see him here. He's a smart bugger!

'A bloody dangerous one,' said another. 'I'd keep well clear if I was you!'

Daniels allowed a sly smile to himself. Like all the others, be damned! But the smile soon faded as he was shown into a cell to share with three others, two of whom were seated on their bunks. They looked at him with interest. He ignored them.

One of them spoke. 'Watcha! I'm Jim Bracken.'

'So?' Daniels glared at him. The other remained silent.

Daniels looked round. The two men occupied both bunks on the left of the cell, the top bunk on the right was stripped of linen, but a book and newspaper were placed neatly on the mattress. Its occupant was elsewhere.

A voice behind him said, 'That's Charlie's bed, he's gone to change the linen.'

Pat removed the book and paper and threw them on to the empty bottom bunk. 'Now it's mine!' he declared and, carefully placing the sheet on it, then the blankets, he climbed up and, sitting with his legs dangling over the side, lit a cigarette.

There was much mumbling from the other two men, which Pat ignored. He was going to make his presence felt from the very beginning. People would need to realize he was not to be messed with.

An exchange of banter outside the cell door announced the imminent arrival of the third inmate.

'Wet the bed again, Charlie?'

'You watch your mouth you cheeky bugger!' And Charlie entered the cell. He immediately saw Daniels sitting on his bunk.

'You're in the wrong bed mate!' he said.

'No, this is the one I like. I don't want someone pissing on me in the night!'

Charlie flushed angrily. 'That was all in fun what you heard. Now get off my fucking bed.'

One of the others grabbed his arm. 'Charlie, this is Pat Daniels!'

Charlie stood glaring at Pat, who could see the man was making up his mind as to what to do next. He waited, staring the other man down.

Eventually Charlie said, 'All right, I don't care where you sleep, but don't push me too far just because I let you get away with this. It's the only time you will. *Capiche*?'

Daniels just gave a mocking smile and lay back on the bed, blowing smoke rings. First round to him.

*   *   *

Victoria was finding Johnny's bodyguard somewhat restricting. She and her lover never seemed to have a private moment, except when they were in bed together and, even then, knowing the man was in the other room made her inhibited and their love life suffered. Curled up in Johnny's arms, she was unable to respond to his mounting passion and pushed him away.

'I'm sorry, darling, I can't.' Getting out of bed she put on a dressing gown and walked towards the door.

'Where the hell are you going?' he demanded.

'To make a cup of tea,' she replied and opened the door.

Johnny sat back against the pillows and sighed. This would never do. He'd have to sort it out. Whilst Victoria was in the kitchen he got out of bed and, walking into the living room, spoke to the man on duty.

'Look mate, I know you've got a job to do but this isn't working. Take yourself home for the night. We'll be fine. The windows are secure and I'll lock the front door behind you.'

'Sorry, Mr Daniels, but I've got my orders. Mr Coleman would have my balls if I left you unguarded.'

Johnny cursed beneath his breath. He'd have to have a word with George. This was too much of an intrusion into his privacy. It was also making Victoria very jittery. He'd call and see him in the morning.

He wandered into the kitchen where Victoria was pouring three cups of tea. He stood behind her, his arms enclosing her, his hand on her breast, nuzzling the back of her neck.

'Be careful,' she warned, 'you'll make me spill the tea.'

He took the pot out of her hand and, turning her round, kissed her, his hand slipping inside her gown.

'Johnny!' she whispered. 'Stop it.'

But he heard the longing in her voice and, lowering his head, he took the pert nipple in his mouth, slipping his other hand between her thighs, his thumb running over her pubic hair.

She moaned softly.

He kicked the door shut with his foot and they slid down on the floor together.

At Wandsworth prison, the inmates were restless. It was visiting day and those men who knew they would see their family or a friend could hardly wait. It was the one time they felt in touch with the outside world. It was the time when the warders were alert and ready for trouble. Not every visit was a success. Those men who were incarcerated always feared that their women were being unfaithful. Some of the wives were finding life difficult and resentment often flared on both sides.

Pat Daniels had no such concerns. All he wanted was to settle the score with his son and was pacing up and down the cell waiting for his head honcho to visit so he could make plans to pay his son back for his betrayal.

Eventually the criminals were led out of their cells to the visiting room. On one side of the room were long tables laid together with chairs on both sides. The inside for the prisoners, the far side for those who came from outside the prison walls.

Pat walked in, his gaze sweeping the chairs of those waiting until he saw Jack Mills, his head man. He hurried over.

'Hello, guv!' said Jack, 'I've left you some tobacco and cigarette papers with the warder and some matches. He said you'd get them later.'

Daniels barely acknowledged this but sat down and, leaning forward in a low voice said, 'Now listen carefully.'

Johnny went to the Club Valletta to see George Coleman and plead his case.

'You've got to give me some leeway,' he said. 'I am grateful to you, George, don't think for a moment that I'm not, but having a man with me twenty-four hours a day is driving me crazy! It's also getting on Victoria's nerves. We don't have any privacy!'

But Coleman wasn't impressed.

'Your father has had time now to make any plan he has in mind to pay you back, maybe even take you out. Doesn't that worry you?'

'Of course it does, I know my old man.'

'Then what are you bellyaching about? Besides, I have to protect Victoria. Every minute she's with you puts her in danger.'

Johnny rubbed his forehead trying to think straight. 'I have told her it would be best if she stayed away from me for a while—' he began.

'But of course she refused,' George interrupted and finished the sentence.

'I'm afraid so,' Johnny agreed. He looked at the other man. 'What can I do?'

'If only we could send her away somewhere,' George suggested. 'I can manage without her. Perhaps I can ask her mother to take her on a holiday. Mind you, we'll have a hell of a time convincing her.' He thought for a moment. 'Leave it with me; I'll have a word with Lily. You go back to work.' He looked over at the man on duty for the day and nodded.

The man walked over to Johnny. 'You ready?'

With a deep sigh, Johnny said, 'Yes, I am, we need to go back to the office.' The two men left the club.

George was about to call Lily when the telephone rang.

'Club Valletta,' he said.

'Hello, is that you, George? It's Bruce Chapman here. Is Victoria around? I want to give her my address.'

'Bruce! You have no idea how pleased I am to hear your voice!'

Later that day, George Coleman paid a visit to Lily, and between them they made plans. George told her of his conversation with Bruce.

'When I told him what was going on between Johnny and his father, the captain had a fit!' he said. 'It seems that Victoria promised him if ever she was in need she'd go out to Malta and stay with him. We need to convince her that if she goes it would help Johnny.' He sighed. 'If only she'd stayed with Bruce, none of this would be happening.'

Lily, as always, came to the point. 'Well, she didn't, which to my mind is a great pity. Johnny Daniels isn't a bad lad but with Bruce she'd have a much better life.'

With a shrug Coleman said, 'That's love for you. Common sense has no place when two people want each other, you should know that, my dear.'

Lily became impatient. 'That was then, this is now. How can we get her there?'

'Bruce said he would arrange it all with his naval links if only you can persuade her it's the right thing to do.'

'I'll come to the club this evening and talk to her,' said Lily. 'She *has* to see sense.'

Their discussion behind closed doors was often heated, as George heard when he walked past the office door a couple of times, but he knew that Lily was as obstinate as her daughter.

Eventually, Lily played her ace card. 'Don't you realize Victoria that your stubbornness is putting the man you confess to love so much in danger?'

Victoria stopped her ranting. 'What on earth do you mean?'

'All the time he's worrying about you, he's letting his own guard down. He needs to be watchful all the time. How can he when you're around?'

Victoria had never considered this and it made her think. Her mother was right, of course. When she was with Johnny, he was always considering her and her safety, worrying about what could happen when she was with him. She'd never forgive herself if anything happened to him because of this.

'But do I have to go so far away?'

'If you stayed here, darling, could either of you keep away from each other?'

Victoria knew they would be unable to do so and eventually she conceded. 'But I want to be able to say goodbye to Johnny first.'

'Of course you do, but please do it here, surrounded by people. You can use the office. Don't go to either his flat or yours. Even with a bodyguard, that's where you're vulnerable.'

Plans were made very quickly. A naval vessel was already taking families to join their husbands as well as stores for the men stationed in Malta and Bruce had secured a place for Victoria among the other wives.

She had packed a case and she and Johnny met at the Club Valletta for their goodbyes.

Tears filled her eyes as her lover walked in and they clasped each other tightly.

'I'm so scared for you,' she told him.

'Then don't be, darling. Being on my own I can make a

few backup plans myself. Dad has only to make one bad move, that's all, and I'll have him, then it'll be all over, I promise.'

He gazed deeply into her eyes. 'I love you and nothing will ever come between us. We're going to have a great life together.'

She saw the determination on his face and kissed him softly. 'If anything ever happened to you . . .'

He placed a finger over her mouth. 'Shh. Nothing is going to happen to me, I can take care of myself, you've got to believe that.' Trying to lighten the conversation he added, 'You just tell that sailor to keep his hands to himself!'

She smiled softly. 'I will. Bruce is a man of honour; he knows you are the only man for me. He just wants me to be safe.'

There was a tap on the door and Lily called, 'There is a taxi here for you, Victoria. It's time to go.'

Victoria threw her arms around Johnny Daniels and clung to him. 'You watch your back!' she urged. 'I want to come back to you very soon.'

He kissed her. 'I'll see you. Take care,' he said and watched her walk to the door. She turned and waved, blowing him a kiss, then left.

Johnny sank into a chair. George Coleman walked in with two glasses of brandy. 'Here, you probably need this more than I do,' he said. 'Now, let the games begin!'

Twenty-Two

Although Johnny was sad to see Victoria go, he was relieved. Now he could concentrate on the task before him, knowing that his father would be plotting some plan or other to get even. He added further securities around his warehouse, putting guards on a twenty-four hour watch. He didn't want anyone messing with his equipment and building materials. When he was at his office, George's man sat outside his door. He was certain now he'd covered all the bases . . . and he waited.

A few days later, he went to examine some work on a

chimney that had been rebuilt. It was a policy of his to check out all finished work before sending his client the bill. His men were totally reliable, but he was a perfectionist, leaving nothing to chance. As usual, he was accompanied by a bodyguard.

When they arrived at the house in question, Johnny picked up the extension ladder that he'd asked to be left for him to make his inspection. He instructed his man to stand at the bottom as a safety precaution and he started to climb. He reached the roof and climbed carefully over the tiles until he was alongside the chimney. As he expected, the men had done a good job and, being satisfied, he slid slowly back to the ladder ready to climb down. He'd only put his foot on the third rung when suddenly it slipped, taking him with it. Johnny managed to grab hold of the sides as he plummeted downwards. It stopped with a shudder, throwing him off. It was pure luck and brute strength that saved him. The man beneath him was thrown backwards on to the ground, with Johnny tumbling on top of him.

Both men sat up, shaken and shocked by the accident.

Johnny was the first to recover. 'You all right?' he asked, slowly moving all his limbs to see if he was injured. His ankle hurt, but appeared not to be broken, but it had already started to swell.

The man got gingerly to his feet, rubbing his thigh. 'Bloody hell, guv'nor, you could have been killed, or at least badly injured. What the hell happened?'

Now on his own feet, Johnny limped away and said, 'I don't know but I'm damned well going to find out!' He picked up the ladder and examined it carefully. He found the screws holding the extended part had been loosened. When he'd climbed to the top, then started his downward journey, he must have moved the ladder enough to unhinge them altogether. Whoever had done this was well aware of his practice of checking out the work and had bided their time until Johnny was due to make his inspection. Only one such person would be responsible and he knew that his father had made the first move.

When he returned to the club that evening, Johnny told George Coleman what had happened.

'You all right?' asked George.

'I sprained my ankle. I went to the outpatients department to check it wasn't broken, they bound it up for me after taking an X-ray. Apart from that we both had a lucky escape.'

'Your old man is a bad bugger. You're his own flesh and blood for Christ's sake!'

With a shrug of his shoulders Johnny said, 'That means nothing to him, he'd sell his own mother if need be, but I am glad that Victoria is now out of harm's way, because, after today, I'm not sure just how far he would go.'

Frowning, George agreed. 'Well, she's in safe hands, Bruce rang to tell me she and the other wives had arrived safely. Now what sort of damage limitation have you arranged?'

Johnny told him about safeguarding the warehouse holding his materials. 'And of course your men are with me at home. In any case, I've added to my personal security.'

George glared at him. 'You haven't been foolish enough to tool up have you? Tell me you haven't.'

Johnny didn't hesitate to answer. 'To be honest, the thought crossed my mind, but no, guns would be foolish, but I have a large cosh by my bed – just in case.'

George gave a sigh of relief. 'Thank God for that! I don't want to see you go down even if you were protecting yourself. But be vigilant, your old man has declared war. However, I've made a few phone calls and soon his little gang will be depleted. Money talks, lad. Especially when the boss is inside.' He smiled slyly. You know the old saying, "when the cat's away, the mice will play?" Well, a few are looking at other options. It'll just take time, that's all.'

'You're a wily old bird, George Coleman,' said Johnny, grinning broadly.

The other man winked at him. 'I know the odd trick or two my son. Between us we'll beat that old bastard!'

Whilst all this mayhem was happening, Victoria had arrived in Malta and was now ensconced with Bruce in an apartment. He had rented it when George and he had arranged for Victoria's visit.

'I of course do have my own quarters at the base,' he told

her, 'but I can always sleep in the spare room, to keep you company.'

'Won't that give cause to local gossip?' she asked with a smile. 'I don't want to be the cause of you losing your good name, Captain Chapman.'

He laughed. 'Things out here are pretty casual when it comes to private lives, darling. In fact, who knows, it could add to my credibility.'

'You know, Bruce, I can't thank you enough for stepping into the breach like this.'

'Didn't I tell you before I left, that if you needed a bolt hole, I was here?'

Her eyes clouded with sadness. 'You did, but never in a million years did I think I would need one and if Johnny and my family hadn't insisted and said I would only add to his troubles by staying, I wouldn't be here now.'

'Is Johnny in real danger do you think?'

'I'm very much afraid so. I met his father once; he is without feeling except for anger and revenge! He'd have plenty of that, but George promised me he'd watch out for Johnny.'

He took her hands in his. 'You really love him, don't you?'

'Yes, Bruce, with every fibre of my body.'

'Then he's a lucky man. Come on, let's take a walk. I'll show you Valletta, you might as well see where your father came from.'

Victoria was sad to see the devastation of her father's home town. Valletta was a port that was integral to the British Empire during the war. Unless they captured Malta, the Axis would lose control of North Africa, which is why the Germans had laid siege to it. The port had suffered as many as four air raids a day by the Luftwaffe but had managed to survive – just. Because of this, King George VI had awarded the island the George Cross. The government had donated thirty million pounds to compensate the Maltese for the extensive war damage and, looking around, Victoria felt they would need every penny.

'I'm pleased my dad isn't alive to see this,' she said to Bruce as they walked around, 'because I'm sure it would break his heart.'

'Well, darling, the Blitz on Southampton didn't break yours,' he reminded her. 'After all, it's what happens in a war, people just get on with it. Malta and all of England will rise from the ashes like the phoenix and rebuild itself. It will just take time.'

They stopped for a coffee at a cafe overlooking the harbour. In peacetime it would have been full of yachts but today it gave a home to an array of naval vessels. The war may be over, but she, couldn't help but feel that it would be some time before all signs of the conflict would be a thing of the past. As they sat talking, Victoria's mind was miles away. She wondered what was happening in Southampton to Johnny.

When they returned to the apartment, she immediately rang George at the club for the latest news. Victoria listened as George Coleman gave her all the details of Johnny's lucky escape. She was horrified. 'Is he hurt?'

'No, love, just bruised. He has sprained an ankle but he's fine, really.'

'What's going to happen next, George? His father won't be satisfied until he feels he's paid him back. How far do you think he'll go, is Johnny's life in danger do you think?'

'No, Victoria.' George lied. 'I don't think he'll go that far. He just wants to teach him a lesson, that's all.'

'I wish I was there,' she said. 'I can't bear being so far away. My place is with him.'

'No, Victoria, it isn't. Johnny will be able to cope with whatever the old man throws at him if he doesn't have to worry about you! Now promise me you won't do anything foolish, like come home . . . not yet a while anyway.'

She reluctantly agreed and had to make the same promise to her lover when she spoke to him later that evening.

'I miss you, darling,' he told her, 'but at least I can relax knowing you are out of harm's way. At least I hope you are!' he teased, trying to make light of the subject. 'I hope that sailor is keeping his hands to himself.'

'Bruce is being a gentleman,' she told him. 'He's put me in an apartment here in Valletta. You would be sad to see all the war damage but, beneath it all, you can see what a lovely place it was and will be again, later when the debris has been cleared and the town rebuilt, like Southampton.' She sighed deeply.

'But I don't want to be here. I just want to be held by you, to feel the warmth of you – to be close to you.'

'I know, sweetheart, and soon you will be, I promise. Now you take care. I'll talk to you soon.'

Three days later, when Bruce was at the base, Victoria went out into the town. Being here was such an opportunity to try and understand her father and his background. She eventually found her way to the local cemetery, with a little help from a couple of the locals directing her. She was amazed at how beautiful it was. All the graves were cared for and bedecked with flowers and some of the gravestones had photographs of the person who was buried there. It didn't seem a bit macabre and in her mind she couldn't help but compare it to the soulless cemetery in Southampton.

The sun was warm and she wandered around reading the headstones, looking at the photos until, to her surprise, she saw the name Teglia on one and stopped to read the carving *Antonio Teglia. Beloved husband and father of Vittorio and Theresa.* Her breath caught in her throat. This was her grandfather and her own father had a sister. She wondered why she had never been mentioned until she saw the headstone next to the grave.

Theresa Teglia. Beloved daughter. Her eyes filled with tears as she looked at the dates. Theresa was only three years old when she passed away. How very sad. But at least she would have known her father for a few short years. She suddenly felt bereft and had to walk away.

Eventually she found herself in a square which enclosed a lawn. On a bench beneath a large tree sat an elderly woman, sheltering from the heat. Victoria walked over to her.

She gestured to the seat and asked, 'May I sit here?' Not knowing if the woman spoke English.

'Please do.' She moved along. 'Are you one of the naval wives?' she asked in perfect English.

Smiling, Victoria said, 'No. But I'm staying with someone from the base.' Looking around she said, 'My father was born here. I try to picture him running around as a small child.'

The woman became interested. 'Really? What was his name?

Only, I was a teacher at the local school, perhaps he was a pupil of mine.'

'Vittorio Teglia,' said Victoria, hopefully.

The woman looked closely at her. 'You are very like your father to look at, my dear.'

'You knew him?' Victoria was delighted.

'Oh yes, he was one of my favourite pupils, so hungry to learn. We used to study pictures of art together. He had a good eye.' She smiled softly as she remembered. 'He had a burning ambition to learn and to do well. But he was a tough little boy, never ran away from a fight – always stood his ground.'

'He died just after I was born,' Victoria told her, 'so sadly I never knew him. He's always been a bit of a mystery to me.' She omitted the murky past of her father, not wanting to dispel the picture the teacher had of Vittorio as a boy.

'The family left here, although I believe his parents returned much later. Sadly I never knew what happened to him. He had a good heart, but I always admired that bit of steel that was his backbone. I always thought it would see him through anything.' She studied Victoria. 'I would say you take after him, you have that same look of determination about you.'

Victoria laughed. 'Well, I can be stubborn!'

'That's character, you, too, can stand your ground, I imagine?'

Victoria was thoughtful for a moment. 'Yes, you're right. I don't usually run away from difficulties, it's not my style.'

'Good for you!' The woman gingerly got to her feet and held out her hand. 'Your father would be very proud of you, I'm sure. It was lovely to meet you, I hope we meet again.'

But as she was left alone, Victoria muttered to herself, 'I doubt that – I'm going home.'

It was visiting day at Wandsworth Prison and Jack Mills was giving his report to his boss.

'I got talking to one of his men in his local pub. He told me he was about to finish his work and was saying how his boss always checked every job and he'd had to leave a ladder for him to climb up to the chimney.' He grinned. 'It's amazing how people will talk over a glass of beer.'

'So what happened?' Pat interrupted.

'I fixed the ladder he would use,' he said, 'loosened the screws so when he used it, it would collapse.'

Pat raised his eyebrows, 'And?'

'He was bloody lucky, guv. He came hurtling down, but managed to grab hold of something as he fell. It was difficult to see from where I was hiding.'

'Was he injured?'

'He was limping, but how he didn't seriously injure himself, I'll never know.'

Pat Daniels cursed beneath his breath. 'Not good enough. Now, here's what I want you to do.'

Sandy was making his usual round of the pubs the following evening, chatting with old friends. When he'd arrived at The Lord Roberts in the Ditches, they'd persuaded him to give them a tune on the piano as he used to do in days gone by. Feeling in a mellow mood, he agreed. It was during his little performance he looked up as the door opened and recognized Jack Mills, Pat Daniels' man. He kept playing but remained vigilant as he did so. A little later, Mills was joined by another man Sandy didn't recognize. The two of them sat together, deep in conversation. Eventually they left together without Mills noticing who was at the piano.

Sandy made his excuses and followed them.

They stopped just below the Horse and Groom and Sandy took cover in the doorway of one of the shops. The stranger took something from inside his coat and handed it over, then walked away.

The Ditches is not well lit at night and Sandy was unable to see what it was the Mills stowed away inside his pocket before he, too, left the vicinity. But Sandy was worried. Jack Mills was an evil man with a record for grievous bodily harm among other things and if he was in Southampton, he was here for a reason and that had to be Johnny Daniels. Sandy hurried off to the Club Valletta to report to George Coleman.

'What did this other bloke look like?' demanded George.

Sandy described him thoroughly having studied him carefully whilst he played the piano. He even noticed the heavy ring the man wore on his right hand.

As soon as he did so, George knew who he was talking about.

'That was Alf Russell, without a doubt. That ring has caused a facial injury in many a fight,' he told Sandy. 'This is not good news, my friend. He deals in firepower. Jack Mills is now tooled up and, if I guess right, with a weapon that's untraceable. Daniels is about to have his son removed permanently.'

'Jesus Christ! George, would he do that?'

The other man shrugged. 'Everything points to it.'

'So what do we do, call the police?'

'And tell them what? You didn't actually see a weapon; we have no proof that Mills is planning a murder. We've got nothing but supposition. They would want proof. We have nothing!'

'Well we can't just stand by and let it happen!' Sandy was outraged.

'Who said we would?'

Sandy was intrigued. 'What had you in mind?'

Twenty-Three

'What do you mean you want to go home?' Bruce was astonished at Victoria's request. 'You've been told that it might not be safe and that Johnny wants you to stay here.' He paced up and down. 'I can't help you to walk back into danger, how could you even ask such a thing?'

'I'm sorry, Bruce. I know I'm putting you in an impossible position, but I have to go. The *Orontes* sails in a couple of days, please get me a berth. If you don't I'll stow away. I've *got* to go home.'

Bruce saw the determination etched on her face and, knowing her as well as he did, knew that no argument on his part would sway her from her decision.

'I think you're absolutely crazy!' he cried.

'But you always knew that, Bruce. You always said it was one of the things about me that you liked.'

He shook his head. 'But, Victoria, darling, this is madness.'

'Yes it is, but I have to go. Please, Bruce, say you'll help me. I've no one else to turn to.'

'You are the most stubborn woman I've ever met! And I know that once you've made up your mind, you will *never* listen to reason!'

Her face lit up with relief. 'Does that mean you'll do it?'

'I'll try, but I don't like it and if anything happens to you, I'll never be able to live with myself.'

She flung herself into his arms. 'Oh, darling Bruce, I do love you!'

'But not enough, sadly. Oh, Victoria, what am I going to do with you?'

'Trust me, I'm not stupid. I know the dangers; believe me I can take care of myself.' She chuckled, 'I wasn't in the navy without learning about survival you know.'

'Oh, if only Johnny Daniels knew what he was taking on with you, he'd run a mile!' was his only retort.

George Coleman wasn't wasting any time. He knew that he had to formulate a plan and quickly. He didn't like the way things were shaping up and no way was he going to let Pat Daniels dispose of his own son.

Although he'd given up his life of crime after Vittorio's death, he'd kept in touch with a number of villains. He was still respected for being the hard man that he was. The fact that he'd gone straight hadn't for one moment been a loss of respect in any way, which stood him in good stead and he was able to call in a few favours, knowing that he wouldn't be refused.

Jack Mills was found and followed wherever he went, his movements reported back to Coleman. George had stepped up the watch on young Daniels so that he was well protected and now they'd have to wait until Mills made his move.

Johnny was well aware of George's arrangements because the other man had shared them with him. But knowing what his father planned was understandably making Johnny very nervous. It was like sitting beneath the sword of Damocles, waiting for it to drop. But he hadn't spent time with Pat in earlier days not to have learned how things worked. There were many ways of hitting a target with firepower. At home, at work, from a distance with a rifle; but he dismissed the latter. Mills was holding a gun small enough to be hidden, according to what Sandy had seen. Or in a crowded place. This option had its weaknesses. The hit man would have to take a chance of getting away in the panic that followed or, being seen, using the firearm again. Johnny dismissed that, too. Mills didn't take chances.

Each day Johnny changed his routine. He left home at different times, took various routes to his office. He never told anyone when he was going to check their work and made sure that if he made a call on a prospective client, the day and time was never made public. He couldn't do any more. The rest was up to George's small army of watchdogs.

This all seemed to be successful as the week passed by without incident, until Johnny was having a quiet drink in the Club Valletta with George and Victoria walked in, the cab driver behind her carrying her case.

The two men looked at her with horror.

'What the bloody hell are you doing here?' Johnny demanded.

'Well, thanks for the warm greeting!' She looked at both of them. 'Sorry, but being in Malta was driving me crazy, so I came home.'

'You shouldn't have done that, Victoria,' George said quietly. 'For once you should have listened to others. Those who knew best.'

When he spoke quietly like that, Victoria knew he was really angry. Even Johnny looked displeased and, shaking his head in despair, said, 'How could you have been so foolish?'

It was only then she realized she'd made a big mistake. 'Sorry, darling, I just needed to be with you.' She gazed up at him, willing him to understand.

'It's not that I didn't miss you, Victoria, I did, like hell, but now you've made things more complicated.' He looked at George. 'What do we do now?'

Letting out a deep sigh George said, 'I'll have to think about it.'

Victoria wasn't a fool, she realized that things were now more serious. 'Right, don't beat about the bush. Tell me what's happening? And *no* lies!'

George gave her all the details, then said, 'So you see, Victoria, you've complicated things considerably. Mills could get to Johnny through you, if we're not careful.'

'Yes, I see. I'm sorry. What do you want me to do?'

Coleman spoke. 'Well, you certainly can't stay at your flat. You'd better stay with your mother for a few days. Don't leave the hotel unless one of my men comes with you.'

'Can I go and pack some fresh clothes? It's cooler here. I've only clothes for a warmer climate.'

George glowered at her. 'Very well. Johnny's man can go with you, then take you to your mother's before he comes back here for Johnny. Now you listen to me and listen good. You do not deviate from anything I tell you. Understand?'

'I promise, I have already made a mess of things. Sorry.' She kissed her lover and followed the man out of the building.

Across the road, her exit was observed by a stranger. A man who'd been brought in from London by Jack Mills. Mills had spent years dodging the law and was very soon aware that he was being followed, but he had made a few other contingency plans which, up to now, had not been discovered. When he was told of Victoria's return, his eyes lit up.

'Well, that *is* interesting,' he said, with a slow, sly smile. 'Keep tabs on her all the time and let me know her movements.' He lit a cigarette. He was a patient man and knew, if he waited, someone would slip up somewhere and he'd be able to strike. Impatience, he had learned, had ruined many a careful plan and he was not going to make any mistakes.

George Coleman had called Lily at the hotel just before Victoria arrived. He had to give her the full picture of what was going on, so she would realize the importance of keeping her daughter safe. She, naturally, was horrified. It was like the old days with Vittorio; days she'd thought she'd left behind when he had died, and now her concerns about Victoria's association with Johnny Daniels had materialized. Mixing with the underworld would always bring problems. It was a way of life. One she hadn't wanted for her daughter, knowing the dangers first hand, and she was furious with Victoria for being so headstrong. A point she made very clear when Victoria arrived at the hotel and was shown into her private accommodation.

'How could you have been so stupid?' She glared angrily at her daughter. 'You knew that it was unwise to return to Southampton. Bruce gave you a safe place to stay, which, under the circumstances, was amazing! Yet you throw all that back in his face to come back to Southampton. I didn't realize how self-centred you were.'

Victoria looked at her mother in astonishment. This wasn't the greeting she'd expected and she didn't know what to say. She tried to explain.

'I had to come back, Mum. I couldn't bear being so far away not knowing if Johnny was safe or not.'

'And now you've only added to his problem! Don't you think he's got enough on his plate without you turning up? Well, my girl, you must now stop behaving like a spoiled brat and do as you're told. Do you understand?'

Victoria felt about five years old. 'Yes I do understand. I'm truly sorry.' She looked crestfallen, but her mother was not impressed.

'You are in the bedroom next door and you can use my sitting room, but you'll have your meals sent up here and not venture into the dining room. You need to keep out of sight. Here you're safe. I'll inform my staff to be wary of the people who come into the hotel, to eye everyone with suspicion.'

'I'm sorry to give you such a problem,' said Victoria. 'I won't be any trouble, I promise.'

'It was only then that Lily relented and took Victoria into her arms and hugged her. 'I didn't want you to be involved in the same world as your father. I wanted to keep you away from all that.'

It was then that Victoria told her mother about finding her grandfather's grave and the woman who had taught Vittorio at school.

Lily smiled as she remembered. 'Despite his way of life, your father was extremely well read and he did have a love of art.

He told me about his teacher who had inspired him. How wonderful that you were able to meet her.'

'What would he have done in the situation we are now in?' asked Victoria.

Knowing that Vittorio would have been ruthless in dealing with Pat's men, who would have probably ended up floating in Southampton's docks, she didn't want Victoria to know this.

'We'll never know,' she said. 'Look, I have to go and work. You get unpacked. There's the newspaper and some books you can read. I'll get the chef to prepare a tray for you. I'll see you later.'

Victoria walked over to the window. The room faced Watt's Park and she watched the locals walking through and driving round, knowing that she had been banned from doing the same. Whereas in Malta she had been free, now she was a prisoner within these walls, through her own foolishness. But in her heart she knew that she'd never have been able to stay away. She needed to be here, to be on top of what was happening. At least she hoped that Johnny would be able to come and see her. She needed to be able to reach out and touch him, to know that he was safe, not to have to wait, miles away, wondering. It would have driven her crazy. She turned away. It was time to unpack.

Her presence at the window had been noted by the stranger, leaning against a tree opposite the hotel, keeping watch. No doubt she wouldn't leave the building today, he thought, so he stubbed out his cigarette and walked away.

A little later, the stranger sat with Jack Mills, trying to figure out a way to fulfil their task.

'Young Johnny is being very smart,' said Mills. 'He knows the score. After all, he was brought up to know how to cover his tracks, to keep safe and George Coleman has him well covered. However . . . now that his girlfriend is back, he is vulnerable.'

'In what way do you mean?'

'He'll want to see her and she obviously wants to be with him or why would she return? Our Miss Teglia is a bit of a firecracker; she has a mind of her own. She won't enjoy being shut in away from her business. Before long she'll be back at the club, mark my words, then we'll have more of a chance.'

'You seem very certain about this.'

'I'd put money on it! Just you wait and see.'

Twenty-Four

Victoria was pacing the floor of her bedroom. It had been three days since she'd moved into her mother's hotel and she was restless. She picked up the telephone and called George Coleman at the club.

'Look, Uncle George, this is ridiculous! I'm like a spare part here doing absolutely nothing, when I could be at the club working.' She heard him sigh.

'So what are you suggesting?' he asked.

'That I be allowed to come back to work. After all, I'll be safe inside the building and you can make sure there is someone with me when I come back here at night.' There was a long silence on the other end of the line. 'Are you still there?'

'Yes, Victoria, I'm thinking.' George knew her for the head-strong woman she was and he knew that if she remained at the hotel she was liable to take things into her own hands, whereas if she were at the club working, he could maintain some control over her.

'Very well. I'll send someone to collect you, but Victoria . . . you must give me your word you won't ever leave the building without one of the bodyguards. It's the only way I can be sure of your safety.'

'Oh, thank you! I promise, really I do.'

'Fine, be ready in half an hour. Wait in your room until the receptionist tells you someone is there to collect you.' He rang off.

Victoria was jubilant. At least now she would feel useful instead of being a drag on everyone and when the call came from the reception she raced down the stairs rather than wait for the lift.

'Let's go,' she told the man who was waiting for her and made for the front door.

He caught hold of her arm. 'Please, wait until I tell you to move.' He walked to the hotel entrance strolled outside, looked around thoroughly, and then beckoned her over as a car pulled up in front of the building with the engine running. He bundled her into the vehicle, getting in beside her.

'Drive!' he told the man at the wheel.

It was then that Victoria suddenly felt the seriousness of it all. This was no game. She was in the middle of something dangerous and menacing. Neither of the men spoke during the journey, but she noticed the driver kept looking in the mirror to see if they were being followed and she wondered if the man sitting beside her was armed. It was like being part of a James Cagney gangster film and she felt goose pimples form on her skin.

When they arrived at the club, she was taken inside at speed. Her escort didn't leave her until she'd been taken to the office where George Coleman was waiting for her.

'Come in, Victoria,' he said. 'Sit down and listen to me.'

Once she was settled he spoke. 'I'm not sure just how serious you are taking all this, but let me assure you that all the plans I've made are for a reason. I'm trying to keep Johnny alive.'

Her eyes widened. 'What do you mean exactly?'

'His father has a contract out on him.'

A wave of nausea swept over her. 'His father wants him dead?'

'Yes. Once Johnny fell in love with you he told his father he was going straight. He told him that he no longer wanted to be part of his way of life and, as you know, he gave the police the information about the stolen books after he found out about the burglary of your flat and the flooding of the cellar. He did this to stop any further moves against you because he wasn't sure just how far Pat would go.'

'Did he think his father would harm me in some way?' Her blood ran cold as she spoke.

'He couldn't be sure, that's why he shopped him. Have you any idea just how dangerous a move this was for him to make?'

'I'm beginning to,' she admitted. 'How is it all going to end?'

'I've no idea at the moment.' He sat back and looked at her. 'I've made a few phone calls to friends and Pat's organization is thinning out every day, but he still has a few faithful members of his gang working for him – it's those buggers we have to watch.'

'Can't we go to the police?'

'No. We have no proof of what may happen, certainly not enough to approach them. We have to handle this on our own, in our own way.'

'Gangland fashion, is that it?'

'If you like to put it that way, yes.'

She looked stricken. 'But you've been straight for all these years; I don't want you to end your life behind bars.'

He chuckled softly. 'Don't you worry about me, love. I'll be fine, it's Johnny we have to worry about.'

'But how long will he be under this threat? It must be driving him insane with worry.'

'Pat has to make a move fairly quickly or he'll lose his authority. We just have to wait. That's why it's imperative that you do as you're told. One false move from you and they'll have a hold over Johnny and there will be nothing more we can do to protect him.'

'I'm so sorry I came back. I now know it was a bad mistake. I'll be very careful, I promise. But I need to work or I'll go mad.'

George rose to his feet. 'That's fine. You'll be safe here. Apart from the doorman I have a couple of men on duty here to keep an eye on things, so you carry on. Act as normal or the punters will wonder what's wrong.' He then brought her up to date with the bookings for the rooms and the restaurant. 'There are a few new members. I've checked them all out, they're legit.' He showed her the membership forms.

Victoria, once she'd been through it all, took a deep breath and went out of the office to look after her customers. Very soon she was back into the swing of things, feeling at last that she was being useful. When anyone commented on her absence, she told them she'd taken a break in Malta for a few days, staying with friends.

During the early evening, Victoria noticed one man she didn't know, sitting quietly drinking beer and reading his paper.

'Who's that?' she asked.

'That's Alec Summers, a new member who's staying with us,' George informed her. 'He joined about a week ago. He's been seconded to the National Provincial Bank to act as manager whilst the proper one is in hospital. I rang the bank to check.'

'You really have been thorough haven't you?'

'It's the only way to keep ahead of the game, love.'

Victoria watched the studious-looking man. He was neatly dressed in a good suit befitting his position, cleaning his glasses very meticulously before returning to his paper.

I bet he's a stickler for detail, she thought, and walked away.

Johnny Daniels was on edge. Despite the fact he was never alone and unprotected and had changed his routine daily, he still felt vulnerable. Even knowing his father for the hard man he was, he still couldn't believe he'd taken a contract out on him. He did think he'd be severely beaten as a punishment if Pat's men had been able to get to him, but that was all and he was prepared for that. But when he'd got the phone call from a member of another gang, who had no time for his father, who'd heard on the grapevine what was going on, he knew for a fact that the man with the job was Jack Mills.

His shoulders ached with tension and he was short tempered. His men had no idea why, of course, although some wondered among themselves why he'd taken on a bodyguard and one or two had voiced their curiosity. He explained it away by saying he always carried a lot of money on him and that seemed to satisfy most. Today, George Coleman had rung him to tell him that Victoria was back working in the club, which only added to his concerns. He decided to go along and see her this evening to make sure she was all right, but if he could, he would persuade her to return to Malta – and safety.

Victoria was delighted to see her lover when he walked into the bar. She rushed over to him and kissed his cheek, but she couldn't fail to notice the circles under his eyes, the drawn look on his face.

'Have you eaten?' she asked.

He shook his head. 'I've been too busy and somehow I don't have much of an appetite these days.'

Victoria took a menu off the bar and handed it to him. 'Right, read this and choose!' As he went to refuse she glared at him. 'You must keep up your strength, darling. You look dreadful and I'm not going to sit back and watch you fade away.'

He sighed and made his choice before ordering a large scotch and soda.

'You look tired, Johnny,' she said, catching hold of his arm.

'I'm not sleeping too well these days.'

'You need someone to cuddle into.' She smiled. 'Someone to hold you in their arms and keep you safe.'

'Oh, I've plenty of people keeping me safe, Victoria, and frankly it's getting on my nerves. I just want to get on with my life!'

She had never seen him like this and it worried her.

After they had eaten she said, 'Come to my office, I need to talk to you.'

Once inside the office, the door closed against prying eyes, he took her into his arms and kissed her. Holding her close, he nestled his face in her neck and breathed in. 'My God, you smell good.' His hand caressed her breast. 'I want you so much,' he whispered.

Victoria closed her eyes and, running her fingers through his hair, said, 'I feel the same.' Then, walking over to a board where all the room keys were kept, she took one down. 'Come with me,' she said and took him by the hand.

They walked upstairs where she unlocked the door of a vacant bedroom and led him inside. 'Now what were you saying?'

Later, as they lay in each other's arms, Victoria spoke. 'How much longer is this going on for? I can see just how the waiting is affecting you and it worries me.'

Johnny heaved a deep sigh. 'I've no idea but I wish it was soon. Then I can move on.'

She didn't know what to say. She could understand how he felt but there was someone who was just waiting for the right moment to try and kill this man who had come to mean so much to her and she couldn't bear the thought. She held him close. What if the killer succeeded? She felt helpless. There was nothing she could do to stop this deadly plan and she hated Pat Daniels with a passion.

Three more days passed without incident. It was surreal, life continued. Johnny went about his business and she continued with hers, being escorted to and from the club, each morning and night. But everyone concerned was living on a knife edge . . . waiting.

On Monday evening it was still early and the club was quiet. Several of the rooms were vacant after the weekend and Victoria was checking to see that the chambermaids had changed the linen, ready for the next customers, when she met Mr Summers leaving his room.

'Good evening,' she said. 'I hope that you have everything you need?'

He smiled at her. 'Thank you, Miss Teglia, everything is absolutely fine. You have a nice place here and I've been well looked after. I'm just going down to the bar, may I buy you a drink?'

'That's very nice of you, I'd be delighted.'

They sat at the bar. The quiet man told her that he travelled from one bank to another, relieving the managers for various reasons. It was his first visit to Southampton and he liked the town.

'I had no idea that it had been so badly bombed,' he told her.

They discussed the Blitz and the war and how the German prisoners had been used to clear the bomb sites whilst they were in the country. Then he excused himself and went to the dining room to eat.

George Coleman wandered over as he left. 'How did you get on with Mr Summers?' he asked.

'He seems a pleasant, unassuming man,' she said. 'He's satisfied with his stay, so that's the main thing.'

'Did he give any indication as to how long he would be staying?'

'No, he didn't say.'

In the dining room, Alec Summers ordered his meal, looked at his watch and thought, after dinner, he really ought to pack his clothes ready to leave. He didn't envisage being here for much longer.

Twenty-Five

The following morning, Victoria was driven to Oakley and Watling, the wholesalers, to order the vegetables for the dining room. Armed with a list from the chef, she climbed out of the car. When the man who'd accompanied her made to join her she stopped him.

'There's no need to come inside with me,' she told him, 'I'll be fine, you wait here. After all, there's nobody following us is there?'

He reluctantly agreed. She breathed a sigh of relief. For once she wanted to be alone, to wander at will, without a shadow. She found it so claustrophobic having someone with her every time she moved out of the hotel or the club. She chose a trolley and began to select the vegetables, placing them on the wooden tray in front of her. One of the assistants helped her to move a sack of potatoes, then left her alone to help herself to the smaller items.

She made her way to the back of the warehouse where she'd been told a fresh supply of cauliflowers had just been unpacked. As she loaded the trolley she was unaware of a figure behind her until something hit her on the back of the head and she slumped to the floor, unconscious.

Victoria slowly opened her eyes. She felt dizzy as she tried to sit up and groaned as the back of her head hurt every time she moved. She put her hand there and winced. She could feel a large bump and as she took her hand away she saw a small amount of blood on it. She desperately tried to gather her thoughts. What the hell had happened? She'd been sorting

out the cauliflowers and someone had hit her! She gazed
around. She was on a camp bed in a small, cell-like room.
The only daylight was from a small grill, high up on the wall.
The door to the cell looked solid. She got to her feet and
staggered over to it and tried the handle. It was locked. She
banged on it with all her might, calling out to anyone who
might be around. There was nothing but silence.

Outside Oakley and Watling, George's man was getting restless.
How long did it take to choose a few vegetables, for God's
sake? Miss Teglia had been over half an hour. He decided to
investigate. When he asked one of the assistants whether they
had they seen her, he was told she was at the back of the
warehouse by the cauliflowers. He walked through, calling her
name, but all he found was the loaded trolley and, lying beside
it, the list from the chef. The back door to the warehouse was
open and he rushed outside, but there was nothing to be seen.
He ran back to the car, yelling at the driver to take him to
the club. Once there, he immediately rushed in to find George
and tell him what had happened at the wholesalers.

'What do you mean, she's missing?' George Coleman thun-
dered. 'How could she be missing? Didn't you stay with her?'

The man nervously told him the whole story and was severely
berated for his stupidity. 'I'm sorry, guv, but she insisted and
I thought she'd be safe. No one was around.'

'Well *somebody* was around! Jesus! Now what?' He picked
up the phone and dialled. 'Johnny, Victoria has been taken.'
He proceeded to tell him what had happened. 'You can expect
a call very soon, my son. When you do, you get in touch with
me right away before you do anything, but don't leave your
office until you hear from whoever has her.'

Johnny Daniels replaced his receiver. He felt sick to his
stomach. So now it was happening – but if only Victoria hadn't
been involved. He prayed that they hadn't harmed her in any
way. Probably not, he thought, as they would use her as bait.
He lit a cigarette and waited anxiously.

Victoria had spent the last half an hour trying to find a way
out of her prison, without success. Even standing on the bed

she couldn't reach the grill. The door was impenetrable and the more she called out the more frustrated she became. Now she was in no doubt she had been taken by Pat Daniels' men and cursed her own stupidity. Why hadn't she been sensible? Had the bodyguard been with her she wouldn't be in this terrifying situation! She sat and waited. Before long, someone had to come.

It seemed ages before she heard footsteps approach and she stood up ready to face whoever opened the door. When she saw her abductor, she could hardly believe her eyes.

'Good afternoon, Miss Teglia.' Alec Summers stood in the doorway, gun in hand.

'You?' For a moment she was speechless.

'I'm afraid so.' He gave a sly smile. 'It pleases me to know that I had you completely fooled. But then, I am good at my job.'

'Which *job* are you referring to?' she asked sarcastically.

'Yes, I know your Mr Coleman checked at the bank. There is an Alec Summers working as a replacement manager, but of course it isn't me. But he was not to know that without going to the bank itself.'

'And what now?' asked Victoria calmly. 'Am I, too, to be a victim of Pat Daniels? I know he doesn't like me.'

'Quite right. You are the cause of his son wanting to leave the organization and, because of you, Johnny shopped his own father.'

'I don't suppose that cold-hearted bastard would understand being in love,' she retorted.

'That's not for me to say.'

'How did you know where I'd be today?'

'I overheard you talking to the chef last night. You said you'd take his order to Oakley and Watling in the morning.' He put down on the floor a sandwich and a cup of water. 'Here, I'm not completely heartless. This will keep you going for a while.' He backed out of the door. 'You may be here for some time.'

'Wait!' She cried. But the door was shut and locked.

She looked at the sandwich. Well, she would eat it to keep up her strength but next time Alec Summers called, she'd be ready for him. She had to do something to get out of here. But just how was she to do it? She had no idea.

The telephone on Johnny Daniels' desk rang. He let it ring several times before picking up the receiver. 'Daniels,' he said – and waited.

'Good afternoon, Johnny.'

'Jack Mills I presume?' he said coldly and heard the soft chuckle at the other end of the line.

'I'm sure by now you will know we have your girl?'

'Yes, you bastard and if you've harmed her in any way, I'll make you pay.'

Mills burst out laughing. 'You are in no position to issue threats to me, sonny boy! Now, you know what I want. We have to meet, Johnny, somewhere quiet. I don't have to spell it out to you, do I? You know what goes down. We can do this the easy way or the other, the choice is yours.'

'What happens to my girl?'

'You play ball with me and we'll let her go.'

'How do I know you'll do so?'

Mills spoke coldly. 'You don't. However, if you are foolish enough to try and double cross me, she'll be the one to suffer.'

Johnny closed his eyes to give himself time to think. 'Fine,' he said eventually. 'You need to give me a few hours to leave my house in order here at the office. Then it'll be my time – my choice of place!'

'It depends where, the time is immaterial.'

'I want to speak to Victoria to make sure she's still alive.'

'You're making a lot of demands for someone in your position.'

'The condemned man is surely allowed some sort of request isn't he?'

He could hear the amusement in Mills' voice. 'Well, if you put it like that. Fine, I'll get your girl to a phone. Stay at your desk, I'll call back in an hour. You can talk to your bird and at the same time give me the meeting place and the time. Don't try and get smart or Victoria will end up floating in the dock.'

Johnny cursed the man but Mills put down the receiver on him. Johnny immediately rang George Coleman.

The ex-villain listened carefully to what had been said. 'Right,' he said. 'I've been on the blower and gathered a few men. Now, Johnny, we have to plan this very carefully. Mills will be expecting you to take some sort of measure, so we have to fool him. There is an old building next to the Empress dock. It's empty at the moment, apart from some old machinery being stored there. It would give my men a place to hide without being seen. It has a large board above it saying Gardner and Sons. Insist on this as its quiet. Make it around eight o'clock tonight.'

'What if he refuses?'

'Then be insistent!'

'What about Victoria? I'm worried about her safety, I don't trust these bastards. If anything happened to her . . .'

'Now, son, you leave that to me, I've got eyes and ears all over the town and we have a bit of leeway time wise . . . We'll find her, I promise!'

George sat at his desk, his mind working, trying to think of the best way to plan ahead. He knew that Mills and whoever was working for him were ruthless. He *had* to have an accomplice because he's been under surveillance all the time by George's men. Coleman came to a decision and picked up the phone.

'This is George Coleman from the Club Valletta; I want to speak to Detective Inspector Bill Cole. It's urgent tell him.'

Ten minutes after his conversation with Coleman, Cole marched into the club, followed by two associates and spoke to George who was waiting for him. They shut themselves away in the office.

'Right! Tell me everything!' the detective demanded. He sat and listened intently. 'I don't like this at all,' he said finally. 'You have no idea where Miss Teglia could be held, I suppose?'

Coleman shook his head. 'We have to find her! I've men searching the dock area already, but I've no idea who else other than Mills is helping him.'

'Why didn't you come to me before?'

'How could I? I had no proof of what was going down.'

'You have to leave this with me now,' said Cole.

'Will I hell! We need every man jack on this. We need to work together if we are to stop Daniels from succeeding.'

Cole stared hard at the ex–villain. 'I won't have a blood bath on my patch, Coleman. Are your men armed? Because if they are, you're breaking the law.'

'Let's just say they are not foolish, but we have to be ready for every eventuality. Mills is armed, we believe, and you know his reputation.'

Cole got to his feet. 'Right, well, here's what will happen. I'll go back to the station to make arrangements. Let me know about the meeting place and the time. Then you leave it to me to place my men. Your men will stand back and let the police do their job . . . understand?'

Coleman nodded.

'In the meantime, someone will be with Johnny Daniels when the call comes through and I'll put out a bulletin about Miss Teglia. Christ! What a mess!' He hurried from the club followed by his men.

Victoria stiffened as she heard voices. She rose to her feet. Obviously, Alec Summers, as she still thought of him, was not alone. There was little she could do but wait. Eventually she heard footsteps coming nearer, then a key was turned in the door and it opened. Summers stepped inside with another man. Victoria felt her blood run cold as she stared into the cruel eyes of the stranger.

'Your boyfriend wants to talk to you,' he said and grabbed her roughly by the arm. 'Now listen to me, girl. Don't try and be stupid or young Johnny will never hear your voice again.'

She remained silent, knowing from his tone that this was no idle threat. But as he dragged her from her cell, she looked around, taking in every detail of her surroundings. This was a small warehouse, now almost empty, she had no idea where, but she could hear the shunting of what sounded like goods trains in the distance. Was she somewhere in the docks, she wondered?

Mills pushed her into an office, which to her surprise looked as if it was in use from the papers littered on the desk. She was pushed into a chair whilst Mills picked up the phone and dialled.

As she waited, through a dirt-stained window she could see a crane, although it did not appear to be in operation. She *was* in the docks, but where?

Mills' voice interrupted her observations. 'Johnny! Here's your girl.' He glared at her. 'Be very careful what you say or it'll be the last time you'll talk to anyone . . . understand?'

With her heart thumping, she nodded. He held the phone to her ear.

'Johnny?' she said, her voice trembling as she did so.

'Victoria? Darling, are you all right?'

She could have cried as she heard his voice. 'Yes, I'm fine, really.'

'Try not to . . .

The phone was taken from her by Mills. 'There you are, Daniels, your bird is still breathing, so what time and where?'

Johnny could scarcely contain his anger. 'You bastard! All right. There's an empty building beside the Empress dock. It's Gardner and Sons. Inside there at eight o'clock.'

Mills thought quickly. 'Right, but *outside* the building and of course I expect you to come alone, that's if you want to spare your girl. She will be in safe hands until I return. If I don't show up, then I don't need to tell you what will happen to her, do I?'

'No you don't. I'll be there.'

Mills replaced the receiver. Looking at Victoria he said, 'I'm pleased you didn't do anything foolish, at least you have some sense.'

'I didn't have much choice, did I!' she snapped.

He laughed. 'Well, you've got some spirit, I'll say that for you.' The smile faded as he dragged her from the chair and both men marched her back to her prison.

'What are you going to do to Johnny?' she cried as she was shoved into the room.

He looked at her coldly. 'Don't be bloody stupid. You know what I'm going to do!' And he slammed the door and locked it.

In Johnny's office, the detective standing with him had been listening in to the conversation. He was deep in thought and frowning.

'Did you hear that goods train in the background?' he asked.

'Sorry,' Johnny answered, 'I was only thinking about Victoria.'

The detective picked up the phone. He gave his boss the details of the meet later that night, then added, 'I'm sure she's in the docks somewhere, guv. I'm positive I heard a goods train in the background.' He listened for a moment and then, turning to Johnny, said, 'I've got to take you to the club. Detective Inspector Cole wants you there until this evening . . . and you're to stay put, he said.'

In the ops room at the police station, men were poring over maps of the dock area, looking at the railway system, marking out squares of territory for a team to search for Victoria. DI Cole had also put in a request for his trained officers to be armed. On the notice board was a mug shot of Mills for the force to be able to identify him during the ensuing raid.

'This man is dangerous and maybe with an accomplice,' the detective warned, 'so be vigilant. I don't want to lose anyone.'

They then planned how to stake out the building designated for the meet.

'Mills is a canny bugger,' he told his men. 'We need to try and think like him. I think he'll get there early. If I was in his situation, that's what I would do, so we'll be there first.'

They gathered round waiting for instructions. The air was full of tension and anticipation. Every man knowing that the next few hours would be critical.

Twenty-Six

Jack Mills was talking to his associate, Fred, also known as Alec Summers. 'We need to plan this very carefully. George Coleman is involved, so I guess he's rounded up a few men to help him out.'

Summers frowned. 'We'll be outnumbered.'

'Only if we stick to the time and place. I don't intend to fall into such a trap. We need to hit young Daniels before he even gets to the docks. It'll be my guess he'll go to the club so he and Coleman can plan their moves.' He lit a cigarette and walked up and down, thinking.

'If I could get on the roof of the building opposite the Club Valletta, it's a narrow street, I would still be in range and take them by surprise. This would give us time to get away. You can be in my car at the back, ready for me, but make sure you keep the engine running.'

Summers smiled slyly. 'Excellent. But what about the girl?'

'Leave her where she is for now. Nobody's going to find her there and I haven't time to waste on her if we're to get into that building. We'll sort her out after. Come on.'

Victoria was pacing up and down the small room in which she was imprisoned. She kept yelling in the hope that someone would hear her cries through the grill, until she was hoarse with shouting. She sank to her knees, exhausted.

She was now convinced she was in the docks, but obviously it wasn't an area which was used much by pedestrians or dockers; otherwise someone would have heard her by now. She pulled her knees up and rested her head against them. Her temples were throbbing, she was chilled with nerves. Her Johnny was in grave danger and she was helpless to warn anyone about it. She prayed he'd told George Coleman what was about to happen; it was her only hope. George was well versed in such matters after spending so much of his life with her father.

Vittorio, the man who had been such a mystery to her. This had been his world! How ugly it was. How could he be the man her mother had loved? How could she have condoned his way of life – have shared in it even? She shook her head, totally confused by such thoughts as she pondered over this.

Johnny, in his earlier days had also been involved in the underworld, full of gangsters, thieves and murderers, until he came to Southampton and fell in love with her and now he was going to pay dearly for it. She wondered if she was to be eliminated too? How could she remain alive? She'd seen the two men, could recognize them. She felt the blood drain from her body, convinced that her time was limited. She got to her feet and started yelling as loudly as she could with what remained of her voice.

Cole rang the club and spoke to George Coleman. 'At seven thirty an unmarked car will collect young Daniels. A couple of my men will be in it. We'll drop him off in the docks well before the meeting time.'

'I'm coming too,' George told him.

'All right, but you stay well back, I don't want to have to worry about your welfare too, I've got enough on my plate.' He omitted to tell him his own men would be placed in the docks much earlier.

George agreed. After all, he had already chosen his men to hide out in the vicinity with orders to do nothing unless it was warranted. They were to be a back up to the police. George knew of course that they would be armed, but they were instructed not to shoot unless it was absolutely necessary, and, if it was, to scarper afterwards. The police would be far too busy to give chase at that moment, so his men would hopefully be safe from prosecution.

George relayed the detective's message to Johnny.

'Has anyone found Victoria?' he asked anxiously.

'Not as yet, son. Give it time. The police and my men are searching the docks, someone will find her, you'll see.' As he lit a cigarette he only hoped that Victoria was found because Mills had said if he didn't return safely . . . well, it didn't bear thinking about and he would have failed to keep Vittorio's daughter safe.

At that moment there was a knock on the door and Sandy walked in.

'Is it right that Victoria is missing?' he asked, wringing his hands nervously.

'Where did you hear that?' asked George with some surprise, as the police had not yet made this information public.

'I heard a whisper. It seems the docks are teeming with police on the search and someone heard her name mentioned. Is it true?'

George told him what had transpired

'Oh, sweet Jesus! That poor child must be terrified.'

'No doubt, but Victoria is made of stern stuff, she'll keep it together. Someone will find her soon enough.'

But Sandy wasn't fooled. He looked at George and just raised his eyebrows. George frowned at him and nodded towards Johnny, who was sitting with his back towards them, stiff with tension.

'When we leave, will you stay at the club, just in case Victoria returns?'

'Yes, yes of course I will.' He lowered his voice. 'This is a bad business, George. I only hope it works out.'

'Don't we all, especially that poor sod,' he said, looking across at Johnny. 'I wouldn't want to be in his shoes right now.' He poured small brandies into three glasses and handed them around. 'Drink up. It'll help settle us all.'

Just before seven thirty that evening, a car drew up in front of the Club Valletta and a constable in plain clothes went inside. The three men were waiting in the foyer. The other officer, armed with a rifle, stood outside the club, waiting.

'I'll walk you out,' Sandy said and went through the door first followed by Johnny, George and the officer.

It had been a dark night but at that moment the moon appeared from behind a cloud and Sandy looked up at it just in time to catch a movement and a flash of light.

'Look out!' he cried and, turning quickly, he grabbed Johnny, pushing him sideways. A shot rang out, quickly followed by another, the second from much nearer by, and a scream of pain filled the night air.

George ran to the figure spread-eagled on the pavement.

'Jesus Christ! That bloody well hurt,' moaned Sandy.

Johnny quickly checked on him before chasing after the two policemen running across the road to the building opposite, who, between them, kicked the door down and entered.

'You old fool!' spluttered George on his knees beside his old friend.

'What the hell happened?' asked Sandy.

'I'm damned if I know. You yelled and sent Johnny flying, there was gunfire and you fell screaming about being hurt.' In the light from the club entrance, Coleman could see blood seeping through Sandy's coat and helped him gingerly to his feet, carrying him inside.

'Call an ambulance, quickly,' he told the barman.

The customers who were in the club began to gather round. 'It's all right folks,' said George. 'The man just had a fall, he tripped over the pavement. Please return to your seats.'

'I thought I heard the sound of gunshots,' said one.

'No, sir, just a car backfiring, nothing to worry about, I assure you.'

When they'd gone George took a couple of linen napkins off one of the tables and, lifting Sandy's jacket, placed them over the wound as a pad to stem the bleeding.

'You'll be all right you old queen, so stop fussing!' But he smiled as he said it. 'You probably saved young Johnny's life tonight and for that we're both indebted to you.'

Meanwhile, in the opposite building, Johnny and the two officers had raced up the stairs to the roof. The marksman held him back. 'Let me go first please, sir.' And he slowly opened the door leading outside. The moon was still shining and they could see a body of a man lying beside the parapet. The officer walked carefully over towards it, closely followed by his associate and Johnny.

Mills was unconscious. The police marksman had hit his target when he'd seen the flash of Mills' gun. One of the men felt for a pulse. 'He's still alive!' he cried.

'Then get on the radio and ask for an ambulance to be sent. We want to keep him that way.' In the distance they heard the screech of tyres as a car took the corner too quickly and crashed.

'Go and check that,' the marksman told his mate. 'It may have something to do with Mills. Call for backup.'

The Royal South Hants Hospital had two unexpected operations to perform in the theatre that night. Sandy had a bullet removed from his shoulder and Mills one from his temple.

In a side ward, Sandy lay back in his bed after he came round from the anaesthetic to find Lily sitting beside him. He looked at her through slightly glazed eyes.

'Lily,' he muttered. 'What are you doing here?'

'Well, hello, my hero,' she said, teasing him, and took his hand. 'I can't leave you alone for a minute, can I?'

'Have they found Victoria?'

Her smile faded. 'No, not yet.'

'Oh dear,' he said and his eyes closed once more.

George Coleman joined Lily. 'I've had a word with the doctor,' he said. 'Sandy's going to be fine. Fortunately the bullet didn't do too much damage. Nothing that can't be treated anyway.'

'What about the other bastard who did this?'

'Ah well, that's a bit different. They managed to remove the bullet lodged in his brain, but they won't know the result until he comes round. At the moment he's stable.' He pulled up a chair. 'The police checked on a car that crashed shortly after the shooting but the driver was and still is unconscious; he's also here under police protection until he comes round. They think he may have had something to do with it and of course they're anxious to question him to find out where Victoria is.'

'Do you think she'll be . . .' She hesitated, faltering over her words, unable to say what she was thinking.

'She'll be fine,' George interceded.

In the dark of the cell in the docks, Victoria Teglia suddenly woke. She'd dropped off to sleep through sheer exhaustion. She felt stiff and cold as she got to her feet trying to gather her thoughts. She had no idea of time and couldn't see her watch face in the dark. She assumed it was late as outside was silent. The trains had stopped running. She sat on the camp bed, wondering how much longer she'd be there before the odious Alec Summers returned with his mate.

She stiffened. Was that voices she heard? She listened intently . . . yes, yes, it was. She stood up and started yelling as loudly as she could. She could hear the voices getting nearer until suddenly a flash of a torch shone through the grill.

'Miss Teglia, is that you?'

Her knees gave way with relief and her voice broke with emotion as she cried, 'Yes it's me! I'm locked in.'

'Don't you worry, miss, we'll soon get you out of there!' came the reassuring reply. 'Just you hold on.'

She burst into tears and collapsed on to the bed.

A short while later she heard the door being unlocked and Johnny's voice. 'Victoria!' And in the light from several torches she saw him as he rushed forward and took her into his arms.

Twenty minutes later a nurse came into the room where Lily and George were sitting beside Sandy. 'Mr Coleman, there's a call for you.'

Lily gazed at him with a look of terror. He gripped her shoulder and left. Minutes later he rushed back in.

'They've found Victoria, she's fine!'

Lily shot to her feet and hugged him, tears running down her face. 'Thank God!'

Victoria refused the police's offer to take her to hospital to be checked over. 'I'm fine, just shaken,' she said. 'I just want to go home.'

Turning to the officer, Johnny said, 'I can't thank you enough. I'll take care of her now. Tomorrow I'll make sure she's checked over by the doctor.'

'If you're sure, sir, then we'll give you a lift.'

In the back of the police car, Johnny just sat with Victoria in his arms until they arrived at her flat. 'Thank you, gentlemen,' he said and, lifting Victoria into his arms, he carried her to her front door.

Once inside, he placed her carefully on the sofa. She was shaking. 'I'm so cold,' she said.

'You're suffering from shock, darling. I'm going to run a hot bath for you then I'm putting you to bed.'

He undressed her and bathed her and then, after making sure she was dry, he wrapped her in a spare blanket and put her into bed, climbing in beside her, tucking the bedclothes around them both. Holding her close, he whispered, 'You're safe now, darling, and you need to sleep.'

'I love you, Johnny,' she murmured and closed her eyes. Within seconds she was breathing softly, oblivious to anything.

Johnny Daniels lay quietly but wide awake, his head full of

images. His father. The close shave with death he'd just had. Sandy taking a bullet that was meant for him – and eventually the safe return of the woman he adored.

At last he would be free of his father. Pat Daniels would no doubt be prosecuted if the police could prove that he had planned the shooting. That would all depend on whether Mills recovered and named his boss. Then there was the driver of the crashed car, yet to be named. Did he have anything to do with the plan and, if so, would he talk? He gave a deep sigh. At least he was still breathing and Victoria was safe. That was enough to be going on with; the rest would have to wait.

Twenty-Seven

At noon the following day, Lily was standing outside her daughter's flat, fidgeting, waiting for the door to be opened, trying to keep control of her emotions. The last thing Victoria would want was a mother weeping with relief. Lily had rung earlier to check that it was all right to call in and Johnny had assured her it was fine. Lily carried a basket with food she'd raided from the kitchen.

Johnny opened the door and ushered her in. 'Victoria is awake,' he told her. 'She's sitting up in bed drinking tea.' He left her alone and, taking the proffered basket and goodies, went into the kitchen.

'Hello, Mum,' said Victoria.

'Hello, darling, how are you?' She saw the dark circles and pinched face and her heart ached. She sat on the bed.

'I'm fine . . . a bit shaken if I'm honest, but so grateful to the police for finding me.'

'I was with George at Sandy's bedside when we got the news you'd been found, it was such a relief.'

'How is dear old Sandy? Johnny told me what happened.'

'He's going to be fine. He was very lucky; the bullet missed all his vital organs and lodged in his shoulder. The surgeons removed the bullet and repaired the damage to their satisfaction apparently. Sandy will have to have some physiotherapy once the wound has healed but he should be fine in time.'

Victoria was gazing intently at her mother whilst she was speaking and Lily, knowing her so well, asked, 'What is it? There's obviously something on your mind.'

'I don't know quite how to put it,' Victoria said.

'Just spit it out, it's always the best way.'

'All right, I will. How could you have lived with my father and shared his life as a criminal? I've now seen that side and I just don't understand.'

Lily was shaken by this outburst. There was a great deal of her past she would never disclose to her daughter, but this needed an explanation if she and Victoria were to continue to be as close as they always were.

'There were many things about your father's life that I didn't condone, but I had no choice. If I went to live with him, I had to take the whole package – and he never pretended to be anything other than what he was. At that time, I was desperate, so I agreed.'

'And after?'

'I fell in love with him.' She shrugged. 'That part I don't have to explain to you. You fell in love with Johnny, knowing *his* background.'

'Did my father ever kill anyone, was he a murderer too?'

'No he was not!' Lily knew at least she was telling the truth. Vittorio had men to do his dirty work and, although she never ever knew the details as he made sure she never questioned him about his business, she did know that he, personally, had never taken a life.

'Vittorio was not like Pat Daniels. All right, he was a self-educated man but strangely, maybe, he did have principles. He was a wise man, a clever one. He took care of me and, had he not died, we were to be married. It was my one regret.' She straightened her back. 'I would have been proud to take his name and you have no need *ever* to be ashamed of it.'

She rose from the bed. 'I've left some food for you with Johnny. Call me if you need anything.' Leaning forward, she kissed Victoria and left the room, with some relief. That had not been what she was expecting.

Victoria picked up the picture of her father from beside the bed and studied the face looking back at her. My mother loved you, she thought. Would I, knowing what you were? I've seen your world and I wonder if I would! I am *not* my father's daughter and that's for sure! She took one last look at the picture and put it away in the drawer of her bedside table.

Several days had passed and Victoria was back at work, as was Johnny. He'd dispensed with the bodyguard, to his relief and was able to work without the feeling of impending doom. Jack Mills was still in intensive care but Fred Black – or Alec Summers, as he'd been known – had recovered consciousness after a few hours and under questioning had rolled over, giving the police all the information they required in the hope of a reduced sentence. If Mills survived he would face a charge of attempted murder and Pat Daniels would again be in court charged with conspiracy. He was now a man alone, without friends or any gang members, who had long disappeared into the dark alleys of the metropolis.

On the following Sunday, George had insisted that Victoria take the day off. 'Go somewhere nice with young Johnny,' he had suggested. And when Johnny came into the club later he told him the same.

'I'll have a word with Victoria and see what she wants to do,' the young man said. But when later he did so, she had other ideas.

'Let's just stay at home in my flat. You can take me there when I finish on Saturday night and we can have a really lazy day.' She smiled mischievously. 'We could spend the day in bed if we wanted to!'

He laughed. 'Are you trying to seduce me?'

'Absolutely!' She snuggled into him. 'I just want to be close to you always. You see, a few days ago, I thought I'd never see you again.'

He tipped her chin upwards so she had to look at him.

'We will always be together! Nothing or no one is ever going to come between us . . . and that includes your sailor boyfriend!'

She chuckled. 'I spoke to Bruce yesterday and told him what

had happened. He'd been so worried about helping me get home and felt so guilty about doing so. As he said, if he'd been firmer, I wouldn't have been in so much trouble.'

'Well, you can't twist me round your little finger like you can him and you'd better know that now. I will be the one who wears the trousers in this relationship, not you!'

She burst out laughing. 'Oh, Johnny darling, you have so much to learn.'

On Sunday morning, after a night of passion, the two of them were curled up in bed. Johnny stretched and yawned. 'Tea I think,' he said and, climbing out of bed, went into the kitchen.

Victoria lay, languid from sleep and sex. How lucky they had been after all, she mused. Things could have been so much worse. Now they had a future free from threat and harm. Of course the court case was before them, which would be unpleasant. Both of them would have to appear as witnesses. Then they could get on with their lives.

Johnny returned carrying a tray with tea and toast on it and Victoria sat up, pulling the sheet around her to cover her nakedness. But Johnny put the tray down and sat beside her.

'It's quite obvious to me, Miss Teglia, that you need a strong man in your life to keep you out of trouble and there is no one better equipped to do that than me!'

She looked somewhat puzzled at his outburst until he held out a small box and, taking her hand, he opened the box to reveal a diamond solitaire.

She looked at him in complete surprise.

'Will you marry me, Victoria?'

For a moment she was stunned. Then she threw her arms around him. 'Oh yes, Johnny, I will, I certainly will!'

When Victoria rang her mother later that morning and told her the news, Lily congratulated her. As Lily said to Luke later, 'At least she has a man who can control her!'

Luke laughed. 'Are you sure about that?'

'To a point, anyway. He's not the man I'd have chosen for her; I thought Bruce would have given her a better life.'

Luke smiled benignly. 'In your opinion! But Victoria is the woman who has to live with him. He seems all right to me.

He's ambitious, doing well in the construction business and, to be honest, I like him.'

George and Sandy were delighted with the news.

'You two were made for each other,' Sandy declared. 'I always had faith in the lad.'

Three months later, Mendelssohn's Wedding March rang out from the organ of St Michael's church and Johnny, with George Coleman as his best man, turned to watch Victoria, on Luke's arm, walk down the aisle.

As she stopped beside him he gazed at her. 'You look beautiful,' he said.

Lily, sitting beside Luke, watched Victoria take her vows. How strange the world was, she thought. The bride was the daughter of Vittorio, a local villain and was marrying the son of one. But thankfully their life would be different. Johnny wanted no part of the world he'd known as a child. He had a thriving business which was totally legitimate and wanted to live a good life with a wife and a family. This he had assured Lily of before the wedding day.

Luke squeezed her hand. 'They'll be fine,' he whispered. You've only got to look at them to know that.'

The wedding reception was held at the Langford Hotel. At Victoria's insistence it had been a quiet affair with just family and friends. Sandy was there, delighted to be witness to the occasion.

'I was honoured to give your mother away the day she and Luke were married,' he told Victoria. 'You were very young then and now look, here you are – all grown up.' He kissed her. 'Be happy, darling. I always knew that Johnny would come good. He'll take care of you.'

'I know he will, Sandy, now you make sure you keep out of trouble!'

'Don't be silly, darling!' He laughed and walked away.

George Coleman watched the proceedings. Vittorio, his old boss, would be so proud of his daughter if he could see her now, he thought. Johnny Daniels looked so happy after all he'd been through with his tyrant of a father. Pat was the one person who still worried Coleman. He was such a devious man and a man who held a grudge. He had that gut feeling about him which was a worry and he never dismissed such a feeling because it had never let him down. He frowned and was lost in thought.

After the speeches and the cutting of the cake, the guests then danced until the bride and groom changed into clothes for travelling.

Victoria hugged her mother and stepfather and kissed them goodbye. 'Thanks for everything,' said Victoria.

'Be happy, darling,' her mother said and kissed her.

The guests watched and waved as the couple left to spend their honeymoon in Devon. The tin cans, tied on to the back of the car, rattled as the newlyweds drove away.

Two weeks later, Pat Daniels walked into the toilets at Wandsworth Prison. The man beside him standing at the urinal zipped up his trousers, washed his hands and left. Two other men entered, standing either side of Daniels. They suddenly lunged at him, both plunging a knife into the villain.

'This is with George Coleman's compliments,' one said.

Daniels slumped to the floor in a pool of blood. The men walked out, closing the door behind them.